Bug Out! Texas
Book 3

Republic in Peril

Robert Boren

South Bay Press

Author/Publishing South Bay Press

Publisher's Note: This is a work of fiction. Names, characters, places, and incidents are a product of the author's imagination. Locales and public names are sometimes used for atmospheric purposes. Any resemblance to actual people, living or dead, or to businesses, companies, events, institutions, or locales is completely coincidental.

Book Layout ©2017 BookDesignTemplates.com
Cover design: SelfPubBookCovers.com/Fantasyart
Bug Out! Texas Book 3– Republic in Peril/ Robert Boren. – 3rd ed.
ISBN 9781973189909

For Fred

You may all go to Hell, and I will go to Texas.

—David Crockett

Contents

Previously - in Bugout! Texas Book 2:

As book 2 opened, the enemy attacked Carrie and Kate at their camp after Jason and Kyle engaged them at the nearby hog blind. The two women put up a valiant fight, but were on the verge of losing when Curt showed up with his Barracuda off-roader, modified with an M-19 Automatic Grenade launcher on the roll cage. After the enemy was defeated, the two couples plus Curt head west.

Juan Carlos and Brendan were stranded on the Mexican side of Falcon lake, but got their boat running again. They had several dangerous missions on the lake as the enemy grew in strength. DPS leadership recognized their potential and used them as testers for new weaponry, including the hand-held SMAW rocket launcher, and later an automatic grenade launcher mounted to the boat and operated by the pilot.

Kelly, Brenda, and Junior made their way west with the enemy hot on their trail. They stopped at a Johnson City RV Dealership for maintenance on Kelly's trailer, and Junior bought a used motor home. They overnighted in Stonewall, then headed west, picking up Rachel on the way. She and her brother were the victims of a road attack. The brother was killed. Rachel decided to stick with Kelly, Brenda, and Junior. They battled their way down the road to Fort Stockton.

Governor Nelson realized that the Federal Government was working against the border states, so he hatched a plan to take Texas out of the union. Kip Hendrix heard the rumors about a new Texas

Republic from Police Commissioner Holly. The Feds caught wind of the plan as well and tried to enlist Hendrix as a spy for the Federal Government. Hendrix recognized that this might lead to his arrest, so he made an overture to Governor Nelson, who was formerly a close friend. They rekindled their friendship and decided to work together for Texas, with Hendrix acting as a double agent.

Eric and Kim snuck into Texas via dirt roads from Louisiana. While they were camped in the woods near Deadwood, they troop transport trucks full of Islamic fighers streaming in. They followed them in the Bronco to see what they were up to. Gunfire erupted, and they watched from a bluff as the Islamists lined citizens up, asking for information and shooting those who wouldn't comply. Eric and Kim opened fire, killing several Islamists. The others took defensive positions and returned fire until local hunters Dirk, Chance, Don, and Kenny joined the fray. They defeated the enemy fighters there, but then the small town of Deadwood came under attack, so the group rushed there to help. They defeated the enemy there and warned the next town of Carthage about Islamists who escaped in their direction. Carthage was ready for them, capturing them when they arrived. Eric and Kim fetched their motor home and continued west, driving to Carthage to spend the night.

Jason, Carrie, Kyle, Kim, and Curt stopped in Sonora, at an RV Park owned by Brushy. They met Gray, his wife Cindy, and their group of bikers there. Gray's group had infected cellphones, and the enemy followed them to Brushy's Park. Curt figured this out just in time to head off disaster. The group killed the Islamists as they attempted a surprise attack on the park. Gray joined Jason's group and headed to Fort Stockton with them. On the way some of Gray's bikers noticed several truckloads of Islamists on the road, so they notified the group, who then set up an ambush, killing them. Brushy showed up to help after his Sonora RV Park was burned to the ground. He joined the group, which made it to Fort Stockton. Nate and Jasper arrived at Fort Stockton and met with Jason's group. Kelly, Brenda, Junior, and Rachel joined them later in the day.

Eric and Kim, still in Carthage, were awakened by artillery fire in the early morning and fled to the west. Deadwood was overrun and most of its residents killed by Islamists. Carthage was shelled. Dirk and his group survived and met Eric and Kim on the road. They joined forces and made it as far as Hearne.

Governor Nelson officially declared the Republic of Texas, causing joy for some Texans and worry for others.

News arrived about the nuclear attacks in New York Harbor and Puget Sound. Kip Hendrix and the others at the State Capital building are herded into the huge underground bunker, where Hendrix, Holly, Ramsey, and Nelson gather with other officials in the situation room to watch events unfold. News of further attacks came, both in the United States and abroad.

Juan Carlos and Brendan were watching the reports of nuclear attacks as well as the US attack on Venezuela when they were warned to flee their base by DPS leadership. Venezuelans forced north by the US Army from Mexico, and were flooding towards them in boats and aircraft. The remaining DPS patrol boats flee towards the dam with the enemy in hot pursuit.

The people at the Fort Stockton RV Park were watching coverage of the nuclear attacks when they heard explosions on the road. Clancy, a resident of the RV Park, climbed onto the roof and saw that a convoy of flatbed trucks carrying M-1 Tanks was being hijacked on I-10 by Islamists. Curt hitched the Barracuda to Jason's Jeep and they raced out to take them on with Kelly, Junior, Kyle, and Gray's men. The women readied their RVs for escape, just in case.

Tanks

C urt made it to his Barracuda, pulling the tarp off and undoing the chains that held it to the back of his toy hauler. He was loading a new belt of grenades when Kyle and Jason ran over.

"Hey, can you tow me behind your Jeep?" Curt yelled.

"Sure, but why?" Jason asked.

"Speed," Curt yelled back. "This only goes about forty-five on the highway. Also I can concentrate on shooting instead of driving."

"Standard hitch?" Jason asked.

"Yeah," Curt said. "I'll pull up behind you."

"I'll get the BARs loaded," Kyle yelled, running to the motor home storage compartment.

Nate, Kelly, Junior, and Fritz arrived, getting their guns out and loading the back of Kelly's pickup truck. Nate got out his BAR.

"Hey, got one too, eh?" Kyle asked when he saw it. "We've got three."

"Hey, Kyle, give the third one to one of those guys," Jason said as he helped Curt hitch up the Barracuda.

"Holy shit, will you look at that thing?" Fritz said, slapping his knee as he stared at the Barracuda.

"We gotta go now," Curt said. "Saddle up."

Jason and Kyle jumped into the Jeep, Curt riding behind in the Barracuda. They drove down the access road to the front gate, waving at their women. Kelly followed, in the cab, with Nate, Junior, and Fritz manning two BARs and other long guns from the bed.

Gray's group came from the other end of the park in a pickup truck, followed by two Harleys. Brushy was riding shotgun with Gray in the cab, the rest of the men in the truck bed.

Jason drove onto I-10 East and punched it. Curt pulled out his phone and called Kyle.

"Curt, what's up?" Kyle asked

"Drive by them and I'll let as many grenades go as I can. I'm going for their vehicles. Then park down the road, and we'll get this baby unhitched. You can let them have it out the passenger side window with that BAR when we go by too."

"Got it, man. Be careful."

"No need to slow down. This gun fires fast. Real fast."

"Okay," Kyle said. He slipped his phone back in his pocket and looked at Jason.

"He said don't slow down as you go by. Pull over and stop a ways past and we'll unhitch. He'll disable their trucks."

"Good, then they won't be able to escape," Jason said.

Kyle got the BAR pointed out the window. "It's gonna get real noisy in here."

"I don't care. Blast the hell out of those bastards We're almost on 'em."

The Islamists were gathering by the first Tank, trying to figure out how to move it away. One of them saw Jason's Jeep with the BAR pointing out the window and yelled. Kyle opened fire, spraying the group with automatic 30-06 fire, and then Curt opened up, firing grenades at their transport trucks as fast as he could aim and pull the trigger, explosions going off every couple of seconds as they went by.

Then more automatic fire from the two BARs in the back of Kelly's pickup truck.

"Pull over there," Kyle said, pointing. "There's a little bluff between us there and the bad guys."

"Okay," Jason said, swerving over and getting behind it. Both of them jumped out of the Jeep and helped Curt get the Barracuda unhitched, as Kelly's truck pulled up behind them.

"Let's drive the Jeep around the other side of this ridge," Jason said. "They'll hide behind the tanks. We'll need a crossfire. We can nail them from back there."

"Good thinking," Curt said as he strapped into the Barracuda. "See you guys afterwards."

"Good hunting," Kyle said.

Curt nodded and took off, rocks and gravel flying out of the big tires.

"What are you guys gonna do?" Kelly asked from the cab of his pickup truck.

"We're gonna get behind them," Jason said. "The Jeep will handle the terrain back there, no problem."

"Okay, we'll go up on foot with the BARs and the other long guns," Kelly said. "Gray and his guys kept going."

"Probably gonna circle back and hit them from the westbound side of I-10," Kyle said. "Watch yourselves. We don't want to lose anybody from friendly fire."

"Yeah, seriously," Kelly said. "You guys watch out too."

Jason drove the Jeep back onto the dirt, behind a small ridge as the explosions of grenades filled the air.

Kyle pointed. "There, man. Let's set the BARs up on the ridge and nail their asses."

"Yeah," Jason said, parking the Jeep. They grabbed their weapons and trotted to the bluff, looking over carefully. Curt drove by again, firing the grenades. The Islamists were yelling in Arabic as they dashed for cover, getting behind the tanks.

"Perfect," Kyle said, dropping the bipod on his BAR. He aimed. Jason did the same.

"Hit as many as you can as fast as you can," Jason said. "When they try to escape they'll run right into Gray and his guys."

Kyle gave a thumbs up and opened fire, Jason joining in, sweeping fire, cutting enemy fighters down as they screamed in panic. Several rushed between the tanks to the other side, and then there was gunfire from that side too, hunting rifles and shotgun blasts.

"Look, they're running east," Jason said, turning his gun and firing at their heels.

"Right into Kelly and Junior!" Kyle laughed as he continued to fire. They heard the other two BARs open up, along with more shotgun and rifle blasts. Then there was silence.

"Think it's over?" Jason asked.

"Yeah," Kyle said, "but keep your eyes open. Might be some of them under those flatbeds or in other nooks and crannies."

Jason nodded and they ran in a crouch, BARs pointed forward. A shot rang out, whizzing by Kyle's head.

"Crap, under the second flatbed," Jason yelled, dropping and sweeping fire underneath it. More fire erupted from the other side of the road. Then silence again. There was the sound of big motors rushing towards the scene.

"Harleys," Kyle said as they got closer. Then yelling in Arabic and two more shotgun blasts.

The Barracuda's engine raced, and two more grenades exploded to the east.

"This ain't over yet," Jason said, rushing to the end of the ruined convoy. There were two troop transports on westbound I-10, one in flames rolling towards the shoulder, the other still coming. Suddenly the cab exploded in flames as a grenade hit, and it rolled to a stop on the center shoulder of the road. Gray's men opened fire on the fleeing Islamists coming out of the canvas-covered back end, Kelly, Junior, Nate, and Fritz joining in. Jason and Kyle sprinted over, dropping and taking aim, spraying 30-06 fire under the trucks, hitting the legs they could see there. The gunfire stopped.

Curt rolled up next to Kyle and Jason. "I think we got 'em all, but I'm going to find a good place to wait for more trucks while the rest of you guys check things out."

"Sounds good, Curt," Jason said. "Nice shooting."

"I would have gone crazier, but I didn't want to damage the tanks. Texas is gonna need those. Made mincemeat of the enemy trucks, though."

"Okay, see you in a few," Kyle said. Curt drove up to the bluff overlooking where the Jeep was parked and turned facing the road.

Jason and Kyle walked over to Kelly and his men.

"Everybody okay?" Jason asked.

"Nobody got a scratch," Junior said

Fritz laughed. "Stupid heathens. They had no idea what was gonna happen to them."

"Yeah," Nate said. "Nice to have all these BARs."

"We got a couple of Thompsons, too, but we left them with the women," Jason said.

"Did you see those crazy guys on the Harleys with those lever-action shotguns?" Fritz asked. "That was some wild shit."

"Gray's guys," Jason said. "They got some AKs too. Captured them down in the Rio Grande Valley, also a few more in Sonora. Glad they're with us."

"Damn straight," Kelly said. "We got ourselves a formidable team."

"That's true, but we're vulnerable," Kyle said. "There's no cover in this damn RV park. They could sweep in from three sides and kill a whole lot of us."

"Yeah, been thinking the same thing," Nate said.

"We should have a meeting on that," Kelly said. "As soon as we get back."

"I second the motion," Kyle said.

"What about the tanks?" Junior asked.

"I'll call Chief Ramsey," Jason said. "He can pass word to the Texas National Guard."

"Good," Kelly said. "We might want to post some guards by these suckers. Sure hate to have the enemy get ahold of them."

"Seriously," Fritz said. "Curt watching for more truckloads?"

"Yeah," Kyle said. "Here comes Gray and his guys."

Gray's truck and two Harleys pulled up next to them.

"That was easier than I expected," Gray said as he got out, joined by Brushy. "Anybody get hurt? We didn't get a scratch."

"We're all okay," Kelly said. "Been lucky so far."

"You don't want to be captured by these guys," Gray said, grim look on his face. "They captured some of our people. Tortured and beheaded them."

"About what I'd expect," Jason said. "Somebody said they've been taking women prisoners, too."

"Yeah," Brushy said. "There were women at my park in Sonora before the attack. They took them away after killing the men. They weren't all young women, either. They ranged in age from about sixteen to seventy."

"Geez," Kelly said. "So they've got a base somewhere nearby."

"Or they used them and dumped them in a ditch somewhere," Junior said. "Bastards."

Jason walked away, phone to his ear after hitting the Austin PD land line contact.

"Austin Police Department," the operator said.

"Chief Ramsey, please," Jason said. "This is Jason Finley."

"Hold the line, please."

Jason waited, looking down I-10 to the east, expecting more truckloads of enemy fighters to arrive. He was still trembling from the battle.

"Officer Finley," Chief Ramsey said. "How are you?"

"I'm good, Chief," he said. "We just got finished with a battle on I-10, just east of Fort Stockton."

"You okay? Lose anybody?"

"We all survived, thank God," Jason said. "The Islamists attacked a convoy. Several flatbed trucks with M-1 Tanks on them. They were trying to figure out how to get away with the tanks when we showed up."

"Geez," Ramsey said.

"Can you contact somebody in the National Guard? Somebody should pick these up before the Islamists come back and try to take them again."

"Can you move them off the road?" Ramsey asked.

"Maybe," Jason said. "Might have shot some of the trailer tires in the firefight. The enemy was using the trailers for cover. Curt was careful not to hit the tanks with his grenades."

"Curt? What does he have?"

"Mark 19 Automatic Grenade Launcher mounted on an off-roader," Jason said. "Works pretty damn well."

Ramsey chuckled. "Oh, brother. I'll make some calls. Don't know if the Texas National Guard can use them. There's a portion of the US Army here. They might be able to pick them up."

"Okay," Jason said. "Thanks."

Jason walked back over to the rest of the group.

"You call the department?" Kyle asked.

"Yeah," he said. "Chief Ramsey knows somebody he can call."

Kyle looked at the flatbed trailers. "Let's go see how they look. Maybe we can drive those trucks out of here."

"Yeah, let's do that," Kelly said.

"We swept 30-06 fire from the BARs under those flatbeds," Jason said. "It'll be a miracle if none of the tires are wasted.

"Hey, man," Tyler said, walking up with Logan. "I worked with M-1 Tanks in the service. So did Logan."

"How come you never brought that up before?" Gray asked.

"Never came up in the conversation," he said. "Let's see if they have fuel in them. We could just drive them over to the RV Park."

Kelly and Junior laughed. "Those would make a worthy addition to our arsenal."

"Yeah, like the Army is gonna let us keep them," Fritz said.

"Let's check them out," Gray said. "At least we can move them somewhere safer than here until they get picked up."

"Yeah, I think that's a great idea," Kelly said.

"Me too," Jason said. "Go for it."

"Gonna need help with the ramps on the flatbeds," Logan said, grinning, his dark brown ponytail swaying in the breeze as he walked. "I'll look at that first one. You take the second, Tyler. Then we'll do the third. I think the fourth one is too messed up. Look at the tracks on the right side."

Tyler nodded, his lanky frame following Logan.

"I'm gonna go too," Kyle said. He followed, Jason and Kelly catching up. The other men stayed put, eyes on I-10 in both directions.

"These trailers are toast, that's for sure," Logan said, pointing at the first flatbed's shredded tires. "BARs didn't do them tires much good." He climbed up on to the flatbed and started pulling the tarp off of the tank. Tyler climbed onto the second flatbed and did the same.

"I'll go help Logan," Jason said, climbing up. Kyle nodded and joined Tyler. They had both tanks uncovered after several minutes of work.

"You need keys for these things?" Jason asked. "Like a car?"

"No, but you need to know the start-up procedures if they've been in storage for a while." Logan got on top. "This is a TUSK-equipped unit. Bitchen." He opened the hatch and lowered himself inside. There was the sound of heavy switches being flipped, and a whirring noise. Then the sound of more rummaging around, more clanking and creaking metal. Logan's smiling face came out of the hatch.

"Well?" Jason asked.

"This sucker is full of fuel, and it's armed, too. All of the machine guns, and the M256 smoothbore. Whoever was transporting these puppies expected them to be in action right away."

"Can you drive it to the RV Park?" Jason asked.

"Hell yeah," Logan said, "and I can teach you guys about them too. That was part of my job in the service. Training."

"You ever in combat with one of these?" Jason asked.

"Nope, that was a game for the young," Logan said. "I was working these at the end of my career. The TUSK setup was just coming in. I'll have to read up on that. It's got remote machine guns which I've never messed with before."

"What is TUSK, anyway?"

Logan smiled. "Tank Urban Survival Kit. Changes to armor and a few other details, like the remote control machine guns - .50 cal and 7.62 mm."

"They didn't have those before?" Jason asked.

"Some," Logan said. "These were set up to drive into cities where there were loads of snipers and people in buildings firing RPGs."

"Oh, I get it," Jason said.

Tyler stuck his head out of the second tank. "Hey, Logan, this thing is ready to go."

"Good," Logan yelled back. Check the third one while I work on getting these ramps put down. Then we should remove the ammo from the busted one and take it with us."

"Who's gonna drive the third tank?" Tyler asked.

"Why don't you show Kyle how to do it?" Logan asked. Tyler looked at Kyle, and he shook his head yes.

"Maybe we should put these at the corners of the RV Park just in case we have visitors," Jason said.

"Damn straight," Logan said. "I'll get you guys checked out on the night-vision systems. There's two on here. Gunner and Commander viewers. We'll see anybody sneaking in after dark. They'll stick out like a sore thumb."

"Good," Jason said. He and Logan climbed off the flatbed.

"Need some help over here," Logan said. "Strong men young enough to do some heavy lifting. You oldsters stand by."

Several of the younger men rushed over, and helped put the ramps in place on the first trailer. Then they rushed over to the second trailer and did the same as Tyler finished with the third unit.

"Hey, Logan, this third one checks out too."

"Good," Logan said. "I'm gonna drive the first one down. Stand back." He climbed up onto the tank and got into the driver's bay. The turbine engine fired up, and he slowly drove the tank down the ramp and turned it towards the road, driving it up towards the ridge where Curt was parked.

"Yes!" Curt yelled, holding is thumb up.

Logan nodded and ran over to the second tank just as the men had finished with the ramp. He drove it off too. He was getting ready to go help with the third when a grenade went off.

"Oh, crap, more enemy trucks," Jason shouted.

"There's about six of them!" Curt yelled, firing off another grenade.

"Tyler, get your ass over here!" Logan shouted.

He ran over, and they trotted to the first tank, Tyler getting into the driver's bay, the Logan into the turret. "Jason!"

Jason sprinted over.

"Get in, man," Logan said. "I'm gonna show you how to load the big gun."

Jason got in. Logan showed Jason how to put on the helmet and then pulled his on. He switched on the intercom.

"Everybody hear me?" Logan asked.

"Yeah," Tyler said.

"I hear you," Jason said.

"Okay, Jason, watch." He opened the breech of the cannon. "See that white door there? Here's how it opens."

He opened the white door across from the breech of the gun. There were cannon rounds in cubby holes, back ends facing out. "Pull out one of the rounds. Then carefully slip it into the breech."

Jason turned, pulled one out, and turned, slipping it into the breech. "Like this?"

"Yes. Notice how that white door closed? Be careful that you don't get tangled up in that. Now push this on the gun to close the breech. Then lean back, because the recoil of the gun is going to send the breech backwards. It moves fast enough to kill you, so be careful."

"Got it," Jason said, closing the breech.

"Tyler, get us up to the road," Logan said, settling into the gunner's seat. He flipped a few switches, then moved the turret towards the target. "Why are those trucks just sitting there?"

"Curt disabled the first two trucks. They're blocking the road, see?"

"Well let's unblock it for them!" Logan said. He aimed the cannon through the sight and fired, the cannon breech moving backwards and then forward as the gun roared. The round broke through the two stopped trucks and hit three of the others. The men outside were cheering.

"We ain't done yet," Logan said. "Load another. Pull the spent cartridge out and put it down there." He pointed to a receptacle near the white door.

Jason followed the procedure and got the second round loaded.

"Okay, let's get closer, Tyler," Logan said. The tank moved forward.

"We should've brought Kyle in here too," Tyler said. "Hard to run these with only three guys. We should be spraying down the whole road with that .50 cal."

"I know, but I can use the 7.62." Logan opened fire, strafing the trucks, Islamists trying to flee the burning wreckage.

"Hey, the last two trucks are trying to turn through the median," Curt shouted. "I don't have a clear shot."

"I do," Logan muttered as he aimed and fired the cannon. He hit the first truck, the explosion taking out the second truck as well.

"That got them, man," Tyler said.

Logan stuck his head out of the hatch. "Any more, Curt?"

"Nah, we iced them all. That last explosion blew shrapnel all over the damn place. Too bad, it probably wasted the ammo they had with them."

"How far down can you see?" Kelly shouted.

"More than a mile, but they were coming fast," Curt said. "That road is a mess now. We're gonna have a back-up. We'd better vamoose."

"Yeah, he's right," Logan said. "At least we'll be able to cross the west-bound I-10. Hardly any traffic going east. We should get across and drive back to the park."

Jason stuck his head out the hatch. "Kyle, follow us so you can drive us back over here to get the next tank," he yelled.

"Wait," Logan shouted. "I'm gonna go get in the second one, and you can follow both of us over there. Then we'll get the third, and grab the ammo out of the last one."

"Sounds like a plan," Tyler said.

Logan got out and ran to the second tank. He got into the driver's bay and pulled up behind the first tank. Tyler drove forward, racing across I-10 and crossing the dusty terrain, getting to the southeast boundary of the RV Park within minutes. He did a k-turn and backed the tank up, it's cannon facing east. When it came to a stop, Jason took off his helmet and climbed out of the hatch, jumping down to the ground as Tyler climbed out of the driver's bay.

"How fast does this sucker go?" Jason asked.

"Hell, it'll go forty under the right conditions," Tyler said. "Maybe faster. Look. If we get any more visitors like that last batch, we could hit them from here easily."

"Yeah, you're right," Jason said, looking. "Good."

The other tank was approaching fast. It went past them, parking on the northeast corner of the RV Park. Kyle roared by in the Jeep, following Tyler's tank and picking him up. Then he drove to the first tank and picked up Jason and Tyler.

"Let's go," Kyle said. He drove back towards the battle site.

"I'll drive the third tank to the southwest corner of the park," Logan said. "I saw a small mound there. I'll be high enough to be able to waste anything coming down either side of I-10. You help the others unload that last tank, okay?"

"You got it," Tyler said. "Wish we had a tanker to take the fuel."

"Me too, but can't have everything," Logan said. "Crap, now I wish you wouldn't have reported these things. We could use them."

Jason laughed. "I could always call them back and say they're all disabled."

"No, man, don't do that," Kyle said. "We need to be on the same side with the good guys."

"How about this," Jason said. "I'll call Ramsey back and suggest that they be left here for a while to protect our position. He could say either yes or no."

"I'm good with that," Logan said. They bounced across the soft shoulders of I-10, the Jeep barely slowing down. "Got to love these Jeeps."

"Seriously," Jason said. "Curt's going to fit this sucker with one of those Mark 19s."

"How's he gonna do that?" Tyler asked.

"Same way he did it with that Barracuda," Jason said. "He's got a 3D printer in the back of his toy-hauler."

"What about the gun?" Tyler asked. "Those don't grow on trees."

"He's got more at his place in San Antonio. As soon as things settle down, we'll be going down there to pick them up."

"That might be a dangerous journey," Logan said.

They pulled up to the other men, who were gathering up enemy guns and ammo that wasn't ruined. Logan got out of the Jeep and raced over to the last tank. The ramps were already up, so he got into the driver's bay and drove it off, heading directly across I-10. Tyler took Jason and Kyle into the last tank, showing them where the ammo was kept, then helping them unload it. Kelly, Junior, Gray, and a few others came over and they passed the 120mm shells from the tank down to Gray's pickup truck. They got the .50 cal and 7.62 ammo after that.

"We about ready to go back?" Kelly asked.

"I think so," Tyler said.

"We'd better go talk to Curt," Jason said.

"Think we need to leave him up there until all of us are out of here?" Kyle asked.

"I'll call Logan," Tyler said. "If he's in a good spot now, we have all the protection we need."

Junior smiled. "Oh, he can see up and down I-10 from one of the tanks?"

"Yeah," Jason said. "C'mon, let's get going."

{ 2 }

Government Cove

The smoke was filling the air quickly, blown about, swirling in the wind.

"Dammit," Richardson said, looking behind them as the temporary headquarters at OPEC Creek burned. "I hope we didn't lose any boats."

"Wonder if we lost a bunch of ammo and grenades?" Brendan asked.

"I saw the supply trucks driving away as we were getting underway," Richardson said. "Unless the enemy took them out on the road, we're probably okay."

"So what the hell are we gonna do in Government Cove?"

"There's a small base there," Richardson said. "Plus anti-aircraft batteries down by the dam. That will give us a little protection."

There was a roar above their heads. "What's that?" Juan Carlos shouted, looking up.

"Yes!" Richardson said. "Those are F-22 Raptors!"

"The US Airforce?" Brendan asked. "Think they're on our side this time?"

"Yeah," Richardson said. "Man those things are fast."

The jets streaked across the sky. A few moments later there were flashes in the water and in the air, not far from the base.

"Looks like they found some targets," Brendan said. "Wow."

More flashes could be seen, further away now, and then the sound of a chopper approached.

"Uh oh," Juan Carlos said.

"That's an Apache," Richardson said. "Probably here to protect us and that dam."

"Hope so," Brendan said. The chopper flew towards them, getting lower.

Richardson got off his gun station, switched the radio on, and changed the channel. "This the Apache? Over."

"Roger that. We're here to escort you to the makeshift docks down by the dam in Government Cove. Over."

"Good. How bad is it up north? Over."

"Really bad. Those F-22s got there in time to stop the attack, but a lot of enemy fighters made it to shore, and we don't have the land forces to stop them. Over."

"So what's the plan now? Over."

"We're evacuating Zapata. Over."

"Son of a bitch," Juan Carlos said. "Really?"

"When are forces expected to show up? Over." Richardson said.

"We don't know yet. Your temporary base will be able to re-supply you. We will get superiority back on the lake with air power, and you guys will hold that. Over."

"Good. Anything else? Over." Richardson said.

"Nope. Over and out."

Richardson put the mic back on the holder. "There you have it."

"How much further to Government Cove?" Brendan asked.

"If we don't have to slow down, about ten minutes," Juan Carlos said. "Hope they've got fuel."

"They will," Richardson said.

There were more brilliant flashes to the north, further away, and an explosion so big that they could feel air rushing at them.

"Wow, what the hell was that?" Juan Carlos shouted.

"Good question," Richardson said. "Ammo dump, maybe."

"Yeah, but we felt it all the way over here. You don't think they lit off a tactical nuke or something, do you?"

"Nah, no way," Richardson said. Just then he saw a huge rolling wave coming at them. "Oh, shit, look at that. Faster!"

"It's already pegged!" Juan Carlos shouted.

"Head for shore now!" Brendan shouted as the giant wave gained on them.

"Son of a bitch," Juan Carlos said. "Look, sandy beach. I'm going in hot. Hold on!" He turned sharply to the left, only slowing down at the last minute, hitting the motor lifters and bracing himself as the boat slid onto the sand, going over thirty miles per hour. They held on for dear life as the boat slowed to a stop. The giant wave rolled towards them, water rising quickly almost to where the boat was, then receding as it rolled past.

"We need to get to higher ground fast!" Brendan shouted.

"No we don't," Richardson said. "Use your head. That wave is gonna take out the dam. We'll be looking at a giant canyon in a couple of minutes."

"Shit," Juan Carlos shouted. "I'm getting up higher to watch." He sprinted up to the end of the sand and climbed up the rock cliff which bounded it, getting high enough to see the lights on the top of the dam. Then they were covered with water, flowing over the top of the dam, a huge cracking noise shacking him. "Oh, my God!" he yelled as Brendan and Richardson ran up the side of the hill to see.

"How many people are on the other side of that dam?" Brendan asked, tears well up in his eyes.

"Not that many," Juan Carlos said. "Some, though. A lot of the water is going to flow onto the Mexican side."

"Look at the shore line dropping!" Richardson said, pointing. "Wish I would have brought the flashlights."

"There's a pretty good moon," Juan Carlos said. "We'd better go make sure that boat wasn't too close to the edge. We got food and water to protect. We're way too far in the middle of nowhere to walk out of here."

"Yeah, we should go check the radio too," Brendan said.

"Don't worry, that Apache saw us," Richardson said.

"What was that?" Juan Carlos asked.

"I don't know," Richardson said. They walked to the patrol boat, laying almost on its side, sand pushed up in front of it. "Careful, this thing might shift. Might even start sliding down into who-knows-what."

Juan Carlos reached in and grabbed the spotlight. He turned it on and pointed it towards the water line. "We're okay. It doesn't drop off for more than a hundred yards. Wonder if the other boats made it out?"

"I'll try them," Richardson said, picking up the microphone. "Turn off that light. It'll drain the battery."

"Okay," Juan Carlos said, switching it off.

"DPS Patrol Boats. Come in. This is Lieutenant Richardson in boat 18. Over."

There was silence for a moment, and then a click. "This is Captain Jefferson. What is your position? Over."

"Thank God you made it, sir," Richardson said. "We turned onto a sandy beach, a couple miles from the dam. Any other boats make it out of the water in time? Over."

"Only one," Jefferson said. "The other three went over the dam. Men presumed dead. Over."

"What was that? Over."

"I don't know, Lieutenant. I need to make some calls. Stay by your boat if you can. Over and out."

{ 3 }

Bunker

Everyone in the situation room sat watching the TV, shell shocked after seeing all the attacks.

"Does this change anything for Texas?" Holly asked.

"You mean are we going to re-join the union?" Nelson asked. "Not yet, but remember that the Republic is only temporary. When it's in the interest of Texas to re-join the union, we will."

Governor Nelson's secretary rushed in.

"What is it, Bryan?" Nelson asked.

"A device was found on a pleasure boat, off Kemah," he said.

There was a murmur around the room.

"We stopped it, though, right?" Nelson asked.

"Just in time, sir. It was a larger device than the one in Puget Sound."

"How bad would the damage have been?" Hendrix asked.

Bryan looked at Nelson.

"It's okay, Bryan. Tell us all what you know."

"According to the team who found it, we would have had extreme damage all the way into Pasadena," he said. "Fallout would have extended into Houston."

"My God," Nelson said. "How we doing on the other checks?"

"Everything is clear between Galveston and South Padre Island, sir," he said. "All marinas are currently closed, and we're setting up inspection points for all incoming ships, commercial and private. They won't get another nuke in that way."

"Thank God for that," Holly said.

"There's something else," Bryan said.

"Go ahead."

"Some kind of device was set off in Falcon Lake. Caused a wave so big that it took out the dam."

"Oh, no," Nelson said. "Loss of life?"

"Minimal, luckily," Bryan said. "Not much population below that dam."

"Well that's something at least. What about our DPS assets?"

"We lost most of the patrol boats and crews, sir," Bryan said.

"Dammit. Was it a nuclear device?"

"Doesn't look like it," Bryan said. "No radiation has been detected."

"Why the hell would the enemy have done that?" Chief Ramsey asked. "Wouldn't this take away an easy crossing point?"

"You'd think so," Nelson said. "I need to talk to DPS Director Wallis. I think we should close this meeting for now and get some shut-eye. We've been up all night. It looks like the attacks are over."

"For now, anyway," Ramsey said. "Should we keep everybody down here?"

"Let's get consensus in the room. Who's in favor of staying in the bunker?"

No hands went up.

"Okay, then let's open the doors back up," Nelson said. "I'd appreciate it if you didn't talk about the foiled attack in Kemah or the explosion at Falcon Lake until we have more information. Especially to the press."

Nelson left the room with Bryan and Chief Ramsey.

"You going home, Kip?" Holly asked.

"Don't know if I can sleep yet," Hendrix said. "Wonder if Maria and Jerry are still in the same room?"

"We'll know in a minute," Holly said. "I'm going home for a while, at least to take a shower. It was like a sauna in there before they got the air conditioning right."

Hendrix chuckled. "Yeah." They walked up the stairs and went into the room where they left Jerry and Maria. People inside were gathering up their stuff, getting ready to leave. Maria saw Hendrix and ran over to him, hugging him, then stiffening and backing away.

"I'm sorry, sir," she said.

"It's okay to be scared, Maria," Hendrix said. "We can leave now."

"Did you see the video on TV?"

"Yes," he said. "Horrible. Just horrible."

"I couldn't believe it," she said.

"Where's Jerry?"

"He left me there," Maria said. "Went to talk to the security team, and never came back." Her eyes welled up with tears.

"You were scared being alone, weren't you?" Hendrix asked softly. "I'm so sorry."

"It's okay," she said. "It's just that I didn't know anybody down there. They all outranked me. I wish I would've been with the other secretaries."

"I didn't know," Hendrix said. "You could've called my cell phone."

"They work down here?" she asked.

"Of course, they have antennas down here, connected to the roof," he said.

"Oh, I guess they'd have to," she said, "but I wouldn't have called you in the situation room. I know you were busy in there."

"Well, that's true," Hendrix said, grim look on his face.

"Something bad happened, didn't it? Something that wasn't on the news."

"I can't talk about it here," he whispered. "I'm sorry. Let's go upstairs."

"Is it really safe?" she asked.

"As far as we know," Hendrix said. "Did you get any sleep last night?"

"No, but I don't think I can sleep now. I'm too worked up."

"Me too," he said. "Let's go to the office. Have some breakfast brought up."

"Okay, sir," she said. They went up the stairs and got into the crowded elevator, riding it to the second floor. Sutton met them in the hallway, a few steps away from the door.

"Where were you?" Hendrix asked.

"Security briefing with DPS and the National Guard. All the mid-level folks were there."

"You shouldn't have left Maria in there by herself," Hendrix said.

"Oh, sir, it's okay," Maria said, sounding embarrassed.

"Sorry," Sutton said. "I thought we'd be right back. They kept us there for the rest of the time."

"It's okay, really," Maria said. They walked into the office suite. "I'll call for some food. You want some too, Jerry?"

"No thanks," he said. "I need to get home and shower. It was too hot down there. Need some sleep, too. If you don't need me, that is."

"Go ahead," Hendrix said. "I'll be out of here as soon as I'm tired enough to sleep."

"But you want breakfast, right?" Maria asked.

"Yes, please," he said. "For you too."

"Thank you, sir," she said. Hendrix nodded and walked into his office, Sutton on his heels. He closed the door after himself.

"I thought you were leaving?" Hendrix said.

"In a minute," he whispered.

"What?"

"Be careful," Sutton said.

"Careful about what?"

"Maria," he said. "You're still looking at her. I know you're trying to hide it. You aren't doing such a good job."

"She's not interested," Hendrix said.

"She softened a little last night. Told me how safe she feels with you." He paused for a moment. "Shit, I shouldn't be telling you that."

"I said don't worry about it," Hendrix said. "I care for her. I'm not going to push her into anything. I learned my lesson."

Sutton stood looking at him for a moment, then sighed. "I hope so. She's scared and vulnerable right now. She'll get over that, and if you've taken advantage, she'll circle back and nail you. Trust me."

"I won't take advantage," Hendrix said. "Really."

"Okay, boss. I'll see you later today."

"You don't have to come back in today. You've been up all night."

"I know, but I can't sleep all day, because then I'll be up all night. I'll nap a few hours, shower, and come in for a while."

"Actually, that's not a bad idea," Hendrix said. "I'll probably do the same."

Sutton nodded and left. Hendrix sat behind his desk, his mind spinning. He wasn't thinking about the attacks.

{ 4 }

Plans for Life

Eric woke to Kim's naked body rubbing up against him in the dim light of dawn.

"You awake?" she asked.

"Yeah, thanks to you," Eric said, eyes barely open, enjoying the feel of her. "You didn't get enough last night?"

"No," she said. "You know how new relationships are. Enjoy it."

"Oh, I have been, believe me," he said, pulling her head close, kissing her gently. Their passion built quickly as they enjoyed each other, ending in sweaty, panting bliss.

"Why so early?" Eric asked, looking at his phone. "It's not even six yet."

"We agreed to leave at seven, remember?"

"Oh, yeah," he said. "I'll get ready. How about breakfast?"

"Cereal okay?" Kim asked.

"Yeah," Eric said. "There's several kinds in the pantry."

"I know," she said, getting out of bed. Eric stared at her. "Take a picture, why don't you?"

"Okay," he said, picking up his cellphone. She grabbed the blanket and covered herself quickly.

"Don't you dare!"

Eric chuckled. "I'm just messing with you. I'll start the coffee maker."

"Good," she said, dropping the blanket as left. She got dressed and joined him, watching the coffee maker heat up. Paco jumped up and down.

"Okay, pal, in a minute," Eric said. "Want to go?"

"We can take coffee, right?"

"Of course," he said. He put a pod in the machine and made a cup for Kim.

"You take that one," Kim said. "Go ahead and get Paco hooked up. I'll be right out."

Eric nodded, grabbing the leash. He went out into the overcast morning, Paco prancing with glee ahead of him. Kim came through the door a moment later with her steaming cup of coffee. They walked down the row of coaches. People were already moving around.

"Something's wrong," Kim said. "I've seen two crying. Lot of grim faces."

"Yeah, there's a bunch of people gathered by the clubhouse," Eric said. "Let's work our way over there and see what's going on."

"Okay," she said. "We can't lollygag, though, if we want to eat and be on the road by seven."

"We could always eat a Clif bar," Eric said.

"True." They got to the crowd of people.

"What's going on?" Eric asked an old man who had tears in his eyes.

"You haven't had the news on?" he asked.

"No, we just got up," Eric said.

"Damn Islamists lit off a bunch of nukes. Floated them into harbors. New York, Seattle, and a bunch of other places."

"Oh, no," Kim said, her body trembling. "In Texas? Or Florida? Or Georgia?"

"No, but there was one in Charleston, South Carolina, and in Ventura, over in California. Oh, and a couple in Russia to."

"My God," Eric said. "We do anything?"

"We're getting ready to bomb North Korea. Evacuations going on around the demilitarized zone and the border with China. We already nuked the hell out of Venezuela."

"Geez," Kim said. "We still a Republic?"

"They ain't said anything different yet," the old man said.

Dirk walked over. "You just now hearing about this?"

"Yeah," Eric said. "I don't have a TV in my trailer. Didn't have the radio on today, either."

"I saw it on my phone browser," Dirk said. "We still leaving at seven?"

"I don't see any reason why not," Eric said. "Do you?"

"No, not really," he said. "The world has gone frigging nuts."

"Yep," Eric said. Kim hugged him, still trembling. "You okay, sweetie?"

"I'm pretty far from okay," she said. "Glad we aren't by the coast."

The old man looked at them. "The Governor said we'd already checked all the harbors, from South Padre Island all the way up to Galveston and beyond. We're safe, and they've locked things down now."

"Good," Dirk said.

A middle-aged man ran out of the clubhouse. "Somebody knocked out the dam at Falcon Lake last night!"

"My God," Dirk said. "Wonder what that's gonna do to the Rio Grande? Might make it easier for the enemy to come across."

Kim looked at Eric, fear in her eyes. "Can we get going?"

"Let's go have breakfast first," Eric said.

"We'll be ready at seven," Dirk said.

Eric nodded, and took Kim and Paco back to the coach. As soon as they got inside, Kim started to sob. Eric took her into his arms. "It'll be okay, sweetie."

"I want to settle down with you and make babies," she said. "I'm afraid the world won't let us."

"Don't worry, we'll be okay," he said, holding her, trying to believe it himself.

Kim fought to get herself under control. "Feed Paco, okay? I think we have time for cereal. I'll get it out."

"On it," Eric said. He kept an eye on her as he tended to the dog. They ate breakfast quickly, barely saying anything.

"What time is it?" Kim asked.

"Ten minutes to seven," Eric said. "I'll unhook the utilities and hitch up the Bronco. You want to stow things in here?"

"Sure," she said.

Eric got up, stood next to her and kissed her forehead. "Don't worry, okay?"

"I'll try," she said. "I'm glad we're together. I'm glad we left Florida, too."

Eric nodded, then turned towards the door and left.

He was just finishing up with the utilities when Dirk and Chance walked up.

"You guys about ready?" Eric asked.

"Yeah," Chance said. "You?"

"I just have to pull the rig out and hitch up the Bronco," he said. "Five minutes."

"Good," Dirk said. "We still gonna try to make Fredericksburg today?"

"Might as well," Eric said. "Hopefully we won't get tangled up getting past Austin."

"We should be okay," Chance said. "Meet you by the gate."

"Sounds good," Eric said. Dirk and Chance walked away, and he went into the coach.

"Ready to pull out?" Kim asked.

"Yeah," Eric said. "You?"

"Go ahead," she said. "Sorry I was such a wreck earlier. You don't need that on top of everything else."

"Don't be silly," he said. He hugged her again, then got into the driver's seat and pulled into the road.

"I'll take Paco for a quick walk while you hitch the Bronco," Kim said.

"Good idea," Eric said. He left, and was half-way through his job when he saw Kim walk away with Paco, her red hair blowing in the breeze. *There's my whole life. Protect her.*

After a few minutes, Eric and Kim rolled up to the front gate. Dirk and his group were already there. They waved and drove out onto the highway.

"Glad to be out of there, and I'm not sure why," Kim said.

"We're liable to see a roadblock or checkpoint when we get closer to Austin."

"Think they'll be able to figure out that we snuck over the border?"

"Nah," Eric said. "I don't see how they could."

"Wow, what are those?" Kim asked, pointing at the oncoming traffic.

"Those look like tanks on flatbeds to me," Eric said, gripping the wheel tighter. The coach rocked as they sped by them. "Geez."

"I counted ten," Kim said. "Maybe we're going to take back the area around Carthage with those."

"Probably," Eric said.

Kim studied his worried face. "Something wrong?"

"Why wasn't there an armed escort with that convoy? Seems pretty crazy with all the enemy fighters around."

Kim thought about it for a moment. "You're right. That doesn't seem right."

"Wonder what kind of tanks they were? Hard to tell with the tarps on them."

"Why does it matter?" Kim asked.

"If they're M-1s, that's probably regular Army."

"Oh," Kim said. "Does the Texas National Guard even have tanks? I don't think the Florida National Guard did."

"Not sure," Eric said. "Either way, it really bothers me that they aren't being guarded. We don't need the Islamists getting ahold of those."

"Here comes more," Kim said. "Another five, looks like."

"Yeah," Eric said, the coach rocking as they flew by. "No guards on those either."

"We need to settle down," Kim said. "Nothing we can do about that now. We'd better watch out for ourselves."

"Okay," Eric said. "Let's talk about something else."

They were silent for a moment.

"You want kids?" Kim asked.

Eric chuckled. "What a question."

"I'm serious," she said.

"But why now?"

"Maybe because of last night and this morning," she said. "I can't believe I'm bringing this up."

"Why do you say that?"

"Because we only just got together," Kim said.

"We've know each other for a while now – even went on a few dates in Florida, remember?"

"We've only just started being intimate," she said. "You know what I mean. Didn't last night and this morning make you think about kids little bit? I felt bonded to you more than ever before."

"I felt the bonding," Eric said. "What you said when you were crying earlier had more of an impact on me."

"I was overwhelmed," she said. "Sorry."

"Don't say that," Eric said. "I understood what you were upset about. It was getting to me too."

"You didn't show it," she said. "You're so hard to read sometimes."

"So I've been told," Eric said. "I guess the answer to your line of questioning is that I do want to have babies with you."

She giggled. "You make me sound like a prosecutor."

"Just messing with you," Eric said. "We haven't been using anything. Birth control, I mean."

"I know, and it's getting to a bad time," she said. "I was on the pill, but like everything else I own, they're back in Florida." She giggled.

"Oh, shit, I didn't even think about that," Eric said.

"We should go to the drug store where we stay tonight. I can get to my doctor on the web portal and have him send the prescription."

"Maybe we shouldn't bother," Eric said, his face turning red right after he said it.

"What?"

"Sorry," he said. "I guess that was a stupid comment."

Kim sat silently for a few minutes, leaning back in her seat. She put her bare feet on the dash and looked over at him. "You were serious, weren't you?"

"It just popped out of my mouth," he said. "As crazy as things are right now, you don't want to be pregnant."

"Don't tell me what I don't want," she said. "You'd be surprised if you could read my mind right now."

"Shit, you want me to knock you up," Eric said. He shot her a sidelong glance.

She giggled. "Knock me up? Really? No way."

"Your mouth sounds appalled, but the look on your face says something different," Eric said.

"You're enjoying this, aren't you?" she said. "Men."

"You brought it up," he said, adjusting himself in his seat.

"Ha ha, I caught you," she said. "If we pulled over right now, you'd be all over me."

"Probably," he said. "If I didn't knock you up this morning or last night, why would it happen now?"

She laughed. "Hell, I could be preggers already."

"No you couldn't," Eric said.

"I'm probably not, but sperm lives for a while, and like I said, I'm getting close to the danger period."

"So what do you want to do?" Eric asked.

"Don't put that on me," she said. "It's not just my decision."

"I didn't ask you to decide, I asked you what you wanted." He watched her face turn red. "You know what you want. You're just afraid to tell me."

"I am not," she said, looking straight ahead.

"Look at me," Eric said.

"Keep your eyes on the road," she said, still looking straight ahead.

"I'm driving just fine," he said, "and I still say you're scared."

She put her arms around her knees and rested her chin on them. "This isn't fair."

"Going for the sympathy play, huh?" Eric said. "Like I said, you brought this up."

She sighed. "Okay, okay. I don't want to go back on the pill. I want your baby in me. That doesn't mean it's a good idea, but it's what I want. There, satisfied?" She looked at him, her eyes wide, pupils dilated.

Eric drove along silently for a couple of minutes.

"Aren't you going to say anything?" she asked, sounding exasperated.

He looked at her, eyes glassy. "I was hoping you were going to say that, but we've got a lot to talk about."

"Oh, my God, you're really head over heels for me, aren't you?" she asked softly.

"I told you I was in love with you already," he said.

"I know, but it didn't hit me like that look just did," she said. "I don't think we need to talk more about this. I'm not going back on the pill, and I'm gonna wear you out every chance I get."

They rode silently down the road, not stopping until they got to Taylor, and then only to gas up and take Paco out. Then it was back on the road, going south on Highway 95, then getting on the westbound 290. In less than an hour they were nearing the 183 Loop.

"Look," Kim said, pointing out the windshield. "That's a huge roadblock. Goes across all the lanes. Dammit."

"They're probably just screening people going into Austin," Eric said. "We're going to the loop, then south to 71. We aren't going into town."

"So why are they stopping people before the southbound loop?"

"Probably the easiest place," Eric said. "Crap, look at that big moving truck."

"What's that guy doing?" Kim asked, voice tremoring.

"He just pushed a couple of cars in front of him past the road block."

"The cops are pulling their weapons," Kim said. "No!"

The big truck stopped after it cleared the roadblock, and then the back door rolled open. There was a tripod-mounted machine gun in the back. It began spewing lead, cutting down most of the cops along the road block and hitting the windshields of the front cars in each lane.

Eric stopped and turned off the engine. "Get out of your seat and crawl to the back of the coach. Hurry!"

She got out and scrambled to the back, Eric and Paco right behind her. Several bullets smashed through the front cab-over window. Kim screamed.

"Stay down! I've got to get to the AKs!"

"No! They'll kill you!" Kim shouted.

"They'll kill us both if we don't do something." Eric crawled to the dinette and lifted the padded seat, grabbing both Ak-47s and the box of ammo. He slapped full clips into both guns. "Stay here."

"Like hell," she said, turning, grabbing the other gun. "I know how to shoot, remember?"

The machine gun was still firing, trying to hit fleeing motorists. Eric slipped out through the front driver's side door and rested his gun on the hood of the car, taking aim and firing, spraying the inside of the truck with lead, killing everybody in there. Then he heard more gunfire. Dirk and Chance ran up on the other side, firing at the Islamists who were searching for cover by the big truck. Don appeared behind them.

"Cover me," he said, rushing forward between the cars, then stopping and throwing a grenade. It rolled under the truck and blew, lifting the back as the Islamists screamed and ran.

"Dammit, I forgot about those," Eric said. Kim got up next to him with her AK and fired several rounds at two Islamists who were trying to get off of the road on the left side.

"Nice shot, honey," Eric said. "I'm gonna go get some grenades."

"Don't bother," Don said. "They're mostly dead. I'll lob a couple more, and then we'll be able to go in." He threw another one, which went into the back of the truck and blew up, shrapnel blowing out the thin sheet metal sides. He ran up further and threw one more, under the front of the truck. It went off, the cab bursting into flame. Three men came out on fire, trying to run away. Kim, Chance, and Dirk shot them before they got very far.

"I think that's it," Don said. "I'm gonna sneak up there. Stay put."

"Be careful, dammit," Chance said.

"I'll call my brother," Eric said. "He's with Austin PD. They'll get somebody out here to take care of this mess in a hurry."

"It's clear," Don shouted as he ran back. "Lot of dead motorists up there."

"I'm calling 911 for ambulances," Kim said.

People were starting to get out of their cars and look around, dazed.

{ 5 }

The Bookmark

Jason, Carrie, and Chelsea were standing next to the tank, looking up at it in the afternoon sun.

"Do you know how to drive that, daddy?" Chelsea asked. "Can you give me a ride?"

"I haven't learned how yet, sweetie," Jason said.

"Don't these things put a big target on this place?" Carrie asked.

"I was worried about that too," Jason said. "They will take out anything coming towards the park, though."

"How'd the owner feel about it?"

"Moe didn't look that happy, but Clancy was excited, since Tyler and Logan are teaching us how to operate them."

"Well, enough of this," Carrie said. "Time to go back. We never had lunch."

"What are we having?" Chelsea asked.

"I don't know, honey," Carrie said. "You can help me pick, okay?"

"Okay," she said. The three of them walked down the bluff, heading to their coach. Kate and Kyle waved at them as they went inside.

"Go have a beer with Kyle if you want to," Carrie said. "It's okay."

"I want to check my e-mail," Jason said. He sat at the dinette and opened his laptop, watching as Carrie and Chelsea puttered around. His phone rang. Carrie looked over at him, startled and scared.

"It's Eric," Jason said, putting the phone to his ear.

"Hey, Eric."

"Jason, how you doing?"

"It's been a busy day. You?"

"I thought we'd be all the way to Fredericksburg today," he said. "Things went a little crazy."

"You okay?"

"We just got into a big battle, on 290 right before the 183 loop."

"On the freeway?" Jason asked.

"Yeah, the enemy pulled a truck up to a roadblock and opened fire with a machine gun."

"Crap," Jason said. "Guess I'll have to watch the news."

"It's not on there yet. I need you to call your boss at Austin PD," Eric said. "And by the way, about fifteen of your brother officers got killed in this thing."

"Oh no," Jason said. "Sure, I'll call Chief Ramsey right now."

"Thanks," he said. "One other thing. Let him know that we've seen several un-guarded convoys on the road. Flatbed trucks with tanks on top, covered with tarps. Those should have security details following them."

Jason was silent for a moment, his head throbbing.

"You still there, Jason."

"We just stopped an attack on a convoy of M-1 tanks, on flatbeds like you're talking about. We just got done bringing the tanks over to the RV Park."

"No, really? Anybody get hurt?"

"Nope, but we were lucky."

"How'd you get the tanks over to the RV Park. You drive the trucks over?"

"There are two guys with us who used to do training on M-1s in the service. They drove them over."

"You call anybody?"

"Yeah, I talked to Chief Ramsey earlier," Jason said. "He was gonna contact the National Guard, and arrange for somebody to pick them up."

"Was there any guards with that convoy?"

"Not that I saw," Jason said, his head pounding harder. "Dammit."

"That's a bad word," Chelsea said. Carrie shushed her.

"What?" Eric asked.

"I'm so stupid," Jason said. "There weren't any drivers there either. No bodies. Only Islamists. None of us thought anything about it."

"This is an inside job," Eric said. "Tell Ramsey. You guys might want to check out the truck cabs a little more thoroughly. I wouldn't be giving those tanks to just anybody who claims to be in the Army, either."

"Yeah, I think you're right," Jason said. "I'll call the chief. Talk to you later." He ended the call.

"What was that all about?" Carrie asked.

"Eric was just in a battle at the junction of 290 and 183," Jason said. "A bunch of Austin officers got killed. He wanted me to call it in to Chief Ramsey."

"It just happened?" she asked.

"Yeah. There was something else. We've been stupid."

"What?"

"Eric has been seeing convoys of tanks on flatbeds like the one we saved earlier. None of them have had a security detail with them."

"There wasn't one with the convoy here, either, was there?"

"No, and we didn't spend any time trying to figure out what happened to the drivers. The cabs were empty but nobody thought anything of it. We were all focused on getting the tanks over here."

"This was an inside job, wasn't it?" Carrie asked.

"May have been. I need to call the chief, and then I think Kyle and I better go back over there and check out the cabs of those flatbed rigs."

"I don't like this."

"Ne neither," Jason said. He hit the Austin PD land line contact on his phone and put it to his ear. It rang twice.

"Austin Police Department," the operator said.

"I need to talk to Chief Ramsey. It's Jason Finley."

"One moment, please."

There was a click a few moments later. "Officer Finley. Something wrong?"

"Two things. First, there's just been a battle at the junction of 290 and 183. My brother was involved. He said there's officers down at a roadblock. Islamic terrorists again."

"Son of a bitch. Just a sec."

Jason heard the receiver being covered by a hand, and the muffled sound of orders being given.

"Okay," Chief Ramsey said. "What else?"

"These tank convoys. My brother brought something up. He's seen several of them on the road. None of them had a security detail. Either did the one that we were involved with earlier."

There was silence on the line for a moment. "We still have infiltrators operating in the Army," Ramsey said quietly. "You get those tanks away from the highway?"

"Yeah. We had to take them off the flatbeds and drive them over here. And by the way, they were full of fuel and ammo."

"This is bad," Ramsey said.

"You make the call about those yet?" Jason asked.

"I tried. Couldn't reach anybody. I'm glad. We need figure this out. Are they in a safe place?"

"They're guarding the RV Park we're in right now. Luckily there are a couple of guys here who know how to operate them. They're gonna teach the rest of us."

"Okay, good. I'll try to get Major General Gallagher on the phone again, but I won't suggest that he send the Army to pick up those tanks. I'll tell him about our concerns."

"Thanks, Chief," Eric said.

"I'd better go deal with this mess at the roadblock. What's your brother's name?"

"Eric Finley," Jason said.

"Good, I'll see if I can chat with him too. He'll probably end up at the station due to this mess."

"Talk to you later, Chief," Jason said. He ended the call. "I need to go talk to Kyle."

"Okay," Carrie said. "You think the DPS is clearing the road yet?"

"Moe called it in, so probably."

"Will DPS want to pick up the tanks?" Carrie asked.

"No, Moe told him we were working with the Army on that."

"Good," Carrie said. "Be careful."

"Don't worry," he said as he left, heading towards Kyle and Kate. Kelly, Brenda, and Junior were just walking up.

"You look worried," Kyle said.

"He does, don't he?" Junior said.

"I just heard from Eric," Jason said. "We need to go back to those trucks and check out the cabs."

"Hey, we never found any drivers, did we?" Kelly asked. "Dammit, how could we be so stupid?"

"Yeah, there was no security detail, and I didn't see shot-up drivers, either," Jason said. "This was a hand off to the Islamists. We got a bad element in the Army."

"Oh no," Kate said, looking at Kyle.

"Did Ramsey notify the Army about those tanks yet?"

"No," Jason said. "He tried, though. Now he's gonna hold off until he can have a private conversation with the head of the Texas Army National Guard."

"Good," Kelly said. "You want to go back to those trucks now, don't you?"

"Yeah," Jason said. "We need to look for evidence about the drivers."

"I'm with you, bro," Kyle said.

"We'll go along and cover you guys," Kelly said.

Brenda and Kate looked at each other, scared. "I thought we were done for the day," Brenda said.

"We're gonna have to get used to this," Kate said. "Mind if I sit this one out?"

"No problem," Kyle said. "Let's take your Jeep, Jason."

"I'll follow you in my pickup," Kelly said. "We better tell the others we're going over there."

"I'll pass the word," Junior said. "Most of the guys are in the clubhouse."

Kelly nodded. "I'll pick you up at the gate. Which guns do you want?"

"Surprise me," he said.

"See you guys over there," Jason said. "Let's grab the BARs just in case."

"Way ahead of you," Kyle said. They grabbed their weapons, loaded them, and drove off in the Jeep.

"We'll have to get on I-10. Can't just go across now. DPS has a lane open already."

"Why is Curt still there again?" Kyle asked as they got onto the road.

"He wanted to take some equipment out of the broken tank," Jason said. "He was muttering something about the FLIR system when we left."

"That's night vision, right?"

"Yeah," Jason said. He slowed as they approached the battle site, and parked next to the Barracuda.

"Hey, Curt, it's us," Kyle yelled.

Curt's head came out of the hatch. "What are you guys up to?"

"We got to wondering about the security detail and the drivers," Jason said. "Wanted to investigate further."

"I was wondering if I was the only one who noticed that," Curt said. "This was an inside job. Somebody in the Army is making these available to the enemy."

"Why didn't you say anything?" Jason asked as he walked over.

"I wanted to have enough time to take everything I need out of this tank, that's why," Curt said. "There's two FLIR systems and a laser range finder in this sucker. Also two remote control machine guns. I'll have to go get a pickup truck pretty soon."

"Kelly's on the way over in his," Kyle said. "Here he comes now."

"Any DPS guys come over here snooping around?" Jason asked.

"Yeah, one guy asked me what I was doing here. Luckily Moe told him we already contacted the Army earlier. I made up a story about waiting for them to arrive."

"Good," Jason said. "We'll go check out the cabs."

"Go for it," Curt said. "I've got to get back to work. We're burning daylight."

Kelly parked next to the Barracuda and the Jeep. He got out with Junior. "What's going on?"

"Curt's going to need some help from you guys," Jason said. "He's taking equipment out of that tank. Needs a pickup truck."

"No problem," Kelly said. "I'm sure he's got some good ideas."

Junior laughed. "Gonna mount that cannon on his toy hauler?"

"Don't give him any ideas," Kyle said, chuckling as he walked towards the first cab. Jason climbed into the second one and got out his little LED flashlight. The cab was clean. Nothing obvious, but he looked everywhere closely. The glove box had only the usual stuff in it. Nothing interesting on the dashboard. He got onto the floor and something caught his eye under the passenger side of the bench seat. An ornate piece of brass sheet metal attached to a reddish-orange braided piece of string. He pulled it out. The sheet metal had a definite middle-eastern look to it. Then it struck him. This was a bookmark. He smiled and slipped it into his pocket. He got out just as Kyle was approaching, on the way to the third truck.

"Anything?" Jason asked.

"Nope, clean as a whistle," Kyle said. "You find anything?"

Jason smiled and pulled the bookmark out of his pocket.

Kyle squinted as he looked closely. "That's a bookmark for a Koran, isn't it?"

"Could be," Jason said. "Let's check the other two."

Kyle nodded and they walked over, Kyle stopping in the third truck, Jason going to the last one.

Jason inspected the last cab. It was clean. As he climbed down he saw Junior and Kelly carrying white boxes with wires hanging out of them to the back of the pickup truck, placing them very carefully behind the cab. "Need some help, guys?"

"Yeah, there's quite a bit more stuff," Kelly said. "You guys find anything?"

"I found something that looks like it might be a bookmark for a Koran, in the second truck."

"I knew it," Kelly said. "Bastards."

"Hey, man, I found something," Kyle said as he walked up. "Paper with a bunch of phone numbers on it. Look." He held the curled-up piece of paper out for the others to see.

"Interesting," Jason said. "Could be nothing. Could be something big."

"Yeah," Kyle said. "How much more stuff needs to come out of that tank?"

"Curt said he needed another hour," Junior said.

"It'll be almost dark by then," Jason said. "Hey, Curt, you want me to hitch your Barracuda up to the Jeep?"

Curt stuck his head out of the hatch. "You confident that those tanks can take on anybody who might show up?"

"Yeah, the one on the bluff is being manned," Kyle said. "We can wait to go back until you're done."

"Good, I could use the help. The remote control machine guns are heavy."

"We'll be right with you," Jason said. Then he looked at Kyle. "I'm gonna take pictures of the evidence and text it to Chief Ramsey. Let's go inside the Jeep for a couple of minutes and get that done."

Kyle nodded and followed Jason.

{ 6 }

Rescue

The beating of the rotors approached, drowning out the rush of the newly flowing river below them.

"There's the chopper," Juan Carlos said, wiping sweat off his brow. "Hear it?"

"About frigging time," Brendan said. "We're almost out of water."

"That's a double-rotor job," Juan Carlos said, pointing.

"They're going to pick up the boat," Richardson said, walking away from the edge.

Brendan looked down into the canyon. "That river probably looks the same as it did a hundred years ago. This is freaky as hell."

"Seriously, dude," Juan Carlos said. "Can't wait to find out what they lit off here."

"Why do they even care about the patrol boat at this point?" Brendan asked. "They've got to have bigger fish to fry."

"They'll probably move us to the Gulf," Juan Carlos said.

"Don't be so sure," Richardson said. "The Rio Grande is a big river. It might still be navigable with these little boats. We've been operating on other parts of the river all along."

"How about down there?" Brendan asked, nodding towards the drop-off.

Richardson laughed. "Hell, that's going to be an unsettled mess for the foreseeable future. It'll take weeks to dry up enough to allow people to climb in and out. At least that will ruin it as a crossing point for a while."

"That chopper is getting loud," Juan Carlos said. "How are they gonna pick up the boat?"

"Straps and chains, probably," Brendan said. "Watched video of that before."

"With these patrol boats?" Juan Carlos asked.

"Nah, bigger boats," Brendan said. "These will probably be easier."

"There it is," Richardson said. "Get ready to fit the slings."

They stood watching as the big chopper hovered, getting lower, the slings dropping slowly towards them from the winch over the side door. Another line dropped, and a man got on the rope and slid down to the beach.

"Howdy," he said, walking over. "I'm Sergeant Reynolds. Ready to get your boat out of here?" He had a helmet and jumpsuit on, wearing heavy gloves.

"Hell yeah," Richardson said. "What do we do?"

"Help me put these slings under the bow and the stern," He said. "We'll have to jockey it a little."

The lapel radio he was wearing scratched to life. "It situated well enough, Reynolds?" the radio said.

"Yeah, Captain," he said while reaching for the first sling. He put it under the bow with help from the others. "Okay, reel it up just a tad."

"You got it," the Captain said. The boat creaked as the sling lifted the front of the boat.

"Hold it," Reynolds said. He grabbed the other sling and guided it under the bow. "okay, up on number two a little."

The boat creaked again as it lifted on the second sling, the first one getting loose.

"Help me pull that first sling back further," Reynolds said. "We'll have to go back and forth until we can get the first sling back far enough towards the transom."

The men helped as the went back and forth, eventually getting the boat about level under the two slings. Reynolds fastened the two straps to the hull so they wouldn't move, and then looked towards his lapel mic. "This looks pretty good. Take her up."

The chopper moved up, the boat going up with it. "Look good, Reynolds?" the Captain asked.

"Roger that. Drop this off and come back to us," he said. "It's just about Miller time."

Juan Carlos and Brendan looked at each other and chuckled.

"Where they taking it?" Richardson asked as they watched the chopper fly away with the boat.

"There's a trailer waiting for it at Government Cove," Reynolds said. "They ought to be back here in half an hour for us."

"Good," Richardson said.

"Pick up many other boats?" Juan Carlos asked.

"No," he said, grim look on his young, stubbly face. "Most of them went over the falls."

"Dammit," Richardson said.

"The enemy took more casualties than we did," Reynolds said. "A lot more. There's a couple thousand bodies down in that canyon. Looks really bad from the air. Kinda like the aftermath of that tsunami in Indonesia."

"Wow," Juan Carlos said. "Gonna stink."

"Damn vultures are already showing up," Reynolds said, sitting on the beach.

"Anybody have an idea what caused the explosion?" Juan Carlos asked.

Reynolds looked at him for a second, then looked away. "Nobody is saying anything. I don't like it. Got a bad feeling."

"It wasn't a nuke, though, right?" Brendan asked.

"No way," Reynolds said. "I was in the air over the water when it blew up. If it would've been a nuke, I'd be dead right now. EMP would have stopped the chopper's engine, and we would've gone over the falls."

"What else has that much power?" Juan Carlos asked. "We don't have any conventional bombs that big, do we?"

"I don't know," Reynolds said, walking to the edge to stare down into the canyon again, looking as far as he could in either direction. "I doubt that the enemy would have wanted to do this. It's just made things harder for them."

"What, you think our side did it?" Richardson asked.

"What's our side?" Reynolds asked. "We aren't part of the USA now. There's been a lot of infiltration into the federal government and the military, from what I've been hearing."

"True," Richardson said.

Reynolds walked back from the cliff. "There's one thing that you might not have heard. That explosion was directional."

"What do you mean?" Richardson asked.

"There weren't shock waves in all directions. Only shock waves in the direction of the dam."

"Dude, that means the dam was the target," Juan Carlos said. "That wasn't a random explosion. Somebody did it on purpose."

"And like I said, a lot more enemy fighters died in this thing than we lost." Reynolds looked at all three of them. "Kinda hard to know who to trust."

"I think I hear the chopper coming back," Juan Carlos said, looking towards the south.

"Wow, faster than I expected," Reynolds said. "Assuming it's our chopper."

They waited as the thumping of the rotors drew closer. Then they saw it descending, slowing, a basket being lowered.

"Who wants to go first?" Reynolds asked, taking hold of the basket.

"I'll go," Brendan said. He hopped in and pulled the strap across the front, locking it.

Reynolds turned his head towards the lapel mic. "Pull it up."

The basket rose quickly, all the way to the door, where a couple of men pulled it in and let Brendan out. Then they lowered it again. The other men followed the same way, Reynolds bringing up the rear. Then the chopper took off for Government Cove, landing in less than five minutes. There were several trucks there, and two patrol boats sitting on trailers.

"Look, there's Captain Jefferson," Juan Carlos said, pointing. The men trotted over to him.

"You guys okay?" Jefferson asked.

"Yeah," Richardson said. "You lose anybody?"

"Not off of my boat," Jefferson said. "We lost almost everybody else, though. Most of them were too far from shore when the wave was coming towards them."

"Shit, man," Juan Carlos said. "What now?"

"Don't know," Jefferson said. "We're still waiting for Wallis to meet with us. He's busy down in the Gulf. We got a lot closer to being hit than the public is being told."

"With a nuke?" Brendan asked.

"Yeah," Jefferson said. "They found one off Kemah just minutes before it was gonna go off."

"Damn," Richardson said. "Glad they got to it in time."

"We were lucky," Jefferson said. "High command is going crazy. The device is small enough to fit in a good sized truck."

"The border still closed?" Juan Carlos asked.

"Yeah, but we have to let some trucks in or we'll start running out of food in a hurry," Jefferson said. "It's a nightmare."

"Maybe we should have thought about that before we seceded," Richardson said.

"We have trade agreements with all of the neighboring states except for New Mexico," Jefferson said. "We left the Federal Government, not the other states."

Juan Carlos looked around as they walked to the headquarters building. "It safe here?"

"Probably," Jefferson said. "We used F-22s and Apaches to smash what was left of the Venezuelan Airforce before we lost the dam."

"You know what that explosion was?" Richardson asked.

"It's classified," Jefferson said. "And no, I don't know."

Submarine Warfare

Chief Ramsey paced in his office, waiting for the conference call to begin. It was running late. Everybody should have been on the line ten minutes ago, but nobody had called in yet. Suddenly his office door opened and Governor Nelson strode in.

"Governor Nelson, I thought you were going to join the conference call," he said.

"Nice to see you, too," Nelson said, smiling.

Ramsey laughed. "Okay, okay," he said. "I'm a little worked up. What about Gallagher?"

"He'll be here any minute," Nelson said. "Wallis too, and Landry."

"Good."

There was commotion outside the office, and the door opened, Wallis, Gallagher and Landry walking in. Ramsey's secretary rushed past them. "Sorry, sir, they wouldn't wait."

"It's okay, Casey," he said. "Hold my calls please."

"She didn't try to stop me," Nelson said.

"She recognizes you," Ramsey said.

"I'd just as soon not be a celebrity," Wallis said. "Sorry we're late. That roadblock attack screwed up 183 and 290. The all the roads in the surrounding area are a mess."

"So sorry about your men, Chief," Gallagher said. Landry and Wallis nodded somberly in agreement.

"We've obviously still got a huge problem in Texas," Nelson said, "even though we dodged the nuclear bullet."

"After seeing the specs on the device, I'm even more worried than before," Gallagher said. "A truck or a train could deliver a bomb pretty easily."

"We won't make it easy for them. One of the reasons we had that big roadblock up was to use radiation detectors," Ramsey said. "Somebody is passing info to the enemy. That attack was aimed at our attempts to protect ourselves from a ground-based attack. They knew what we were trying to do, and sent us a message."

"Nothing got through that roadblock after they attacked?" Gallagher asked.

"No," Ramsey said. "They shot up the first few cars in every lane. Nobody could get through. We have a lot of eye-witnesses."

"Yeah, some eyebrows got raised when you hauled everybody within visual distance to the station," Wallis said. "They still here?"

"We're still conducting interviews," Ramsey said, "but we've already let a lot of them go."

"Let's get this rolling," Gallagher said. "I've got a lot to do today."

"Me too," Wallis said.

"Okay, gentlemen," Ramsey said. "Have a seat in front of the big-screen there."

The men sat, swiveling their chairs to view the flat screen TV on the wall next to the door. Ramsey got behind his desk and worked his desktop. A picture came on the screen. It was a piece of brass sheet-metal, cut and shaped in an ornate manner. A braided piece of string was tied to it.

"What is that?" Nelson asked.

"I know what it is," Gallagher said. "Saw those in the Iraq war. That's a bookmark for a Koran. Where'd you find it?"

"One of our officers found it under the seat of an Army transport flat bed, just outside of Fort Stockton."

He switched the picture to a strip of paper with about twenty phone numbers on it.

"What's that?" Wallis asked.

"Phone numbers," Ramsey said. "All from burner phones. Found in the cab of one of the other trucks in the same convoy."

"Okay, we need some details, so stop with the dramatics," Gallagher said.

"I'm getting there," Ramsey said. "Been trying to call you for the last several hours, Major General Gallagher."

"I've been busy," he said. "Sorry."

"It's okay. Better to have all of us together on this anyway," Ramsey said. "So here's the story. Remember my two officers who were involved in that Superstore attack?"

"Yeah," Wallis said. The others nodded.

"I put them on paid leave and told them to disappear after the Islamists tried to kill them. They ended up in Fort Stockton with men who fought alongside them at the Superstore attack."

"Go on," Gallagher said.

"They heard the attack on the military convoy from the RV Park they're staying at, just off I-10 by Fort Stockton. They went to the aid of the convoy. Ended up killing all of the enemy fighters."

"What was the convoy for?" Wallis said.

"Transport of four M-1 A2 tanks, equipped with TUSK," Ramsey said.

"Holy shit," Gallaher said.

"You didn't know these were being transported down I-10, did you Gallagher?" Nelson asked.

"No," he said. "If this was legit, I would have heard about it from General Walker or General Hogan."

"That's what I was afraid of," Ramsey said. "We have enemy infiltration at Fort Bliss."

"There are some Muslims who are legitimately in the US Army, you know," Wallis said. "Aren't we jumping to conclusions here?"

"I don't think so," Ramsey said. "The bookmark and the burner phone numbers together are too much of a coincidence. Then there's the fact that there was no guard detail with the convoy, and the fact that the drivers of the trucks were not killed – by the bad guys, that is. They were killed in the battle, by our guys."

"Our guys meaning your two Austin PD officers and a bunch of rednecks?" Wallis asked.

"Yeah," Ramsey said. "And by the way, those rednecks, as you call them, saved a lot of lives during the Austin terror attack, remember?"

Nelson held up his hands. "Let's not start fighting over this. Go on."

"Okay, sorry," Ramsey said. "I've got an eyewitness account of several more convoys similar to this one, driving east with no security detail. We have elements of the US Army passing these vehicles to the enemy. Need I remind you what a number of TUSK-equipped M-1 A2 tanks could do to our cities?"

"Son of a bitch," Gallagher said. "Who else knows about this?"

"Just you guys and the people involved in the battle at Fort Stockton."

"How about the eyewitness?" Wallis said.

"You're about to meet him. He's just down the hall."

Ramsey pushed a button on his phone. "Casey, call Officer O'Reilly and tell him I'm ready."

"Why bring him in here?" Wallis asked.

"He's been all over the backroads of east Texas," Ramsey said. "And by the way, he's the guy who tipped us off about the cellphone tracking."

Officer Sam O'Reilly came in with Eric and Kim, both of them looking nervous.

"Welcome," Ramsey said. "Have a seat."

"You're my brother's boss, aren't you?" Eric said.

"Yes," Ramsey said. "This is Eric Finley and his girlfriend Kim."

Eric nodded to the group. Kim looked at them, forcing a smile.

"Well, what did you see and where?" Gallagher asked.

Ramsey stood behind his desk. "Wait a minute. Let's tell him who we are. That's Major General Gallagher of the Texas Army National Guard. Next to him is Major General Landry of the Texas Air National Guard. The big gentleman across from them is DPS Director Wallis. I'm sure you recognize Governor Nelson."

Eric nodded, still looking nervous. He cleared his throat. "Glad you're all here. We've got a big problem."

"Thanks for being here," Nelson said.

"We didn't exactly have a choice," Kim said.

"Sorry," Ramsey said. "We're worried about a nuke being driven into Austin, after looking at the device we found in Kemah."

"You found a nuke in Kemah?" Eric asked. "Shit."

"It was small enough to slip into a truck," Ramsey said. "That's why we had the roadblock up. We were scanning vehicles as they went through."

"That's a worse problem than I'm going to tell you about," Eric said.

"Understand," Ramsey said. "Please go on. What have you seen?"

"We saw convoys of military flatbeds with tanks on them, going eastbound without any security escort," Eric said.

"How many?" Gallagher asked.

Kim pulled her cellphone out and looked at her notes. "Twenty-three so far."

"Holy shit," Wallis said. "Why would they be heading east?"

"The enemy was coming across the border from Louisiana," Eric said. "We encountered them and fought with them east of Carthage."

"Know where they're crossing over?" Wallis asked.

"West of Longstreet, Louisiana," Eric said. "Small dirt roads, leading from there to Deadwood."

"And how did you run into them?" Gallagher asked. "That's a remote area."

Eric glanced at Officer O'Reilly, and he nodded yes.

"Kim and I got stopped at the Texas border outside Houston," Eric said. "We were coming to help my brother bury my dad and avenge him."

"Avenge him?" Wallis said.

"Yeah," Eric said. "Anyway, when we got turned away at the border, we went north until we could find a place to drive across."

"You're a Texan, though, aren't you?" Nelson asked.

"I was born here, but I'd been living elsewhere for a few years. Last place was Florida. Didn't matter at the border. They wanted proof that I was a resident. I didn't have any."

"Don't worry, you're in no trouble with us," Nelson said. "Quite the contrary."

"We've got a real problem around Carthage," Gallagher said. "And Deadwood is a ghost town now. Lots of people got killed. Not many escaped."

"Some of the Deadwood folks are with us," Eric said. "Dirk, Chance, Don, Francis, and the others. In the holding cell."

"You'll be allowed to leave soon," Ramsey said. "All of you."

"How did you find out about the cellphone tracking?" Wallis asked.

"We noticed we were being followed east of Grand Cane, Louisiana," Eric said. "Tried to lose them. No dice. I saw a chance to ambush them just west of Longstreet. After we killed them, I looked at a cellphone left in the cab of their truck. The tracking program was still running."

Nelson looked at Ramsey. "This related to the Austin PD phone problems?"

"Yes," Ramsey said.

"It fixed?" Wallis asked.

Ramsey sighed. "We aren't sure, to be honest. We swapped out all the bad phones, but we don't know who placed the virus, or how they did it. It's possible that our new cellphones are already compromised."

"Dammit," Wallis said. "We should talk about what happened in San Antonio."

"Go ahead," Ramsey said.

"Let's finish with the civilians first," Wallis said.

"Don't worry about them," Nelson said. "What's on your mind?"

Wallis sat silently for a moment. "Okay. The enemy fighters who took over the San Antonio City Hall used cellphones to find the mayor and city council members. All of them were hidden, using shelter-in-place procedures we had put into place just a week before."

"So the phones there were compromised too," Nelson said. "Crap. They could be listening in on our conversation right now, couldn't they?"

"It's possible," Ramsey said.

Gallagher looked at Eric. "How'd your phone get compromised?"

"I talked to my brother," Eric said. "The virus got onto my phone from his. And by the way, it only took one conversation. We hadn't talked for months before that."

"He called because of your father, didn't he?" Ramsey said. "Sorry to hear about that."

"Thanks," Eric said.

"So where do we go from here?" Nelson asked.

"Put out an APB on the tank situation," Ramsey said. "Stop any further tank convoys, and attempt to find the ones that went east."

"I'll be going to Fort Bliss as soon as this meeting is over," Gallagher said. "Time to change my plans."

"Want me to tag along?" Landry asked.

"Sure," Gallagher said.

"Can we go now?" Eric asked. "I need to join my brother."

"Of course," Ramsey said. He looked at Officer O'Reilly. "Let the people from Deadwood leave with them, too, okay?"

"Got it," O'Reilly said. He got up and headed for the door, Eric and Kim behind him. Gallagher and Landry left too. Nelson and Wallis stayed behind.

"You two got something else to discuss?" Ramsey asked.

"Yeah, and this one does have to stay in the room," Wallis said.

"Go ahead," Ramsey said.

"We know what knocked down the dam at Falcon Lake," Nelson said, grim look on his face.

"What?" Ramsey asked.

"It was a new Russian anti-submarine weapon," Wallis said. "Moscow contacted us as soon as they heard what happened. Somebody stole the prototype and engineering data a couple of years ago."

"Son of a bitch," Ramsey said. "Who did it?"

"Venezuelans, working with the North Koreans, from what I've been hearing," Wallis said. "It's all pretty hush-hush at the moment. Kinda good this happened. It helped us to open a back-channel with the CIA and FBI."

"Why would the enemy do that?" Ramsey asked. "It wasn't a strategic plus for them. It ruined one of their best border-crossing points."

"The CIA thinks it was a warning to our subs," Wallis said. "The North Koreans think that's how we'll hit them."

"Maybe they forgot about our B-2s," Ramsey said.

"They think that DC has lost control of the Air Force," Wallis said.

"They'd be right, but they've also lost control of the Navy," Ramsey said.

"Yes, all of that is true," Wallis said. "The US Airforce will attack North Korea. It's going to happen soon. That's not why we're telling you this."

"Uh oh," Ramsey said.

"We have reason to believe there are more of these devices in Texas," Nelson said. "We need to start surveillance on all of our major reservoirs."

Ramsey plopped back down in his chair. "Lake Travis. Walter E. Long Lake. Lady Bird Lake. Hell, Canyon Lake isn't that far away. Lots of people around all of those."

"Yeah, well I'm on my way to the Dallas-Fort Worth area next," Wallis said. "You know the situation they have."

"Lewisville Lake," Ramsey said, looking down at his desk. "My God."

"There are others in the Dallas area too," Nelson said. "There are lakes all around the city."

"I'll get people on Lake Travis and Lady Bird Lake right away," Ramsey said. "Those two are the biggest threats to us. Lady Bird Lake might wash out the Airport if it's hit."

"Agreed," Nelson said. "Let me know if you need additional resources."

"You can bet on that," Ramsey said. He stood and shook hands with Wallis and Nelson. They left the office, and Ramsey went back to his desk. He hit the button on his phone.

"Yes, sir?" Casey asked.

"Contact my leadership team," he said. "Meeting in the big conference room in half an hour."

{ 8 }

Pasture

It was almost over. Kim and Eric were relieved.

"Sorry we had to hold you up," Officer O'Reilly said as he walked Eric and Kim down the long hallway to the holding area. "We'll get you and your friends out of here right away."

"Nobody messed with our vehicles, I hope," Eric said.

O'Reilly chuckled. "We didn't take your AKs or your grenades," he said. "And by the way, I know Jason and Kyle. Tell them Sam says hi."

"I was wondering," Eric said. "What happens to the tanks?"

"They ones your brother and his friends captured?" Sam asked.

"Yeah."

"Chief Ramsey told them to hold onto the tanks for now," Sam said. "Here we are." He unlocked the door and led the Eric and Kim inside. Dirk and Chance stood.

"Well?" Dirk asked.

"We're out of here," Eric said.

"Where's Francis?" Kim asked.

"A couple of officers wanted to chat with him about Deadwood," Don said.

Francis's wife Sherry stood trembling, looking at Sam. "Go get him right now. Please." She was a handsome woman of about fifty-five with gray hair. The two younger women got next to her, putting their hands on her shoulders.

"This is scary," said Alyssa, a slim redhead with a face of delicate beauty, about nineteen.

"He'll be okay, Alyssa," Don said to her.

"You sure, dad?" she asked. "Seems like everybody wants to shoot at us or take us prisoner."

"It's getting old," said Chloe, the other girl, who had short black hair and a pixie face.

Alyssa sighed. "Well, at least we didn't disappear from town, Chloe. I hope Shelby is okay."

"Francis will be here in a couple minutes," Sam said. "You guys can gather up your stuff."

"Where are our vehicles?" Chance asked.

"Impound yard, right next door," Sam said. "I had somebody replace that broken window in the Class C."

"Wow, really?" Eric asked. "Thanks for that."

"Don't mention it," Sam said. "I knew we'd be letting you go pretty soon. We need you guys in the battle."

"So why'd we have to be in that meeting?" Kim asked.

"The Chief thought he'd have trouble convincing everybody we had a problem with the tanks," Sam said. He shook his head and chuckled. "I told him that wouldn't be a problem."

Francis walked in. "Hey, guys. We ready to hit the road?"

Sherry rushed over and hugged him, tears streaming down her face.

"It's okay, sweetie," he said. "I was just chatting with some fellow law-enforcement officers, that's all."

Eric smiled at him. "You look happy."

"Just talked to one of my deputies. He and the other dozen people who escaped to the east survived," he said. "I was afraid they were dead or captured."

"That's great!" Don said.

"Is Shelby with them?" Alyssa asked.

"She is," Francis said. "She was lucky. Some of the other girls had a worse time."

"They still in Louisiana?" Chance asked.

"For now, yeah," Eric said. "The enemy attacked Longstreet. Did the same thing there that they did in Deadwood. Beheaded men, took women hostage. Our guys notified the Louisiana State Police, who found them pretty quick. Killed them with the help of some of our folks. Liberated a bunch of women they'd taken hostage, too. Some of them were from Deadwood. Lisa Sanders and Britney Howell, among others."

"What were they doing with them?" Chloe asked.

Francis got a grim look on his face. "Sex slaves."

"Ewww," Alyssa said, looking up at Don with fear in her eyes. "Daddy."

"We'll protect you," Don said, pulling his daughter into his arms.

"Let's get out of here," Eric said, trying to shake the disgusting images out of his head.

"Follow me." Sam led them down the hall and out into the parking lot, crossing the side street into the impound yard. He used his key card to open the gate. Their vehicles were there, along with many other vehicles from the roadblock battle. Some of them were from the first row, shot up and bloody.

"My God," Kim said, looking at them. "How many people died there?"

"Fifteen officers and about forty civilians," Sam said. 'We killed eight Islamists and two Venezuelans."

"Geez," Eric said, walking up to his rig. Paco was inside, jumping up and down. "Thanks for keeping the windows open." He opened the side door and Kim went inside

"We had the air conditioning running earlier, and gave him some water," Sam said. "I thought that little guy was going to attack me."

Kim giggled. "He's a killer." She squatted just inside the door and patted her thighs. Paco ran up and jumped on, licking her arms and face.

"Hey, pal," Eric said, reaching down to pet his head. Paco looked up at him, eyes alive, tail wagging. "I'd better feed him something before we leave."

"We should take him out," Kim said. "There might be an accident or two in here."

"Maybe," Eric said.

"Where should we go?" Dirk asked, standing outside his rig with Chance and Don.

"I don't think we'll make it to Fredericksburg," Eric said as he put the leash on Paco. "Let's check Dripping Springs. I know of a small park that usually has a few spaces open. It's not nice, but it's off the beaten path. Good place to rest."

"Know their number?" Kim asked.

"No, but I know where it is. I'll search for it and get the number, okay?"

"I'll take the leash," she said.

Dirk checked his rig, looking for bullet damage on the truck and the trailer behind it. Francis checked out his Suburban.

"We didn't see any damage other than the window on the class C," Sam said. "You guys were lucky."

"Yeah, looks okay," Dirk said. "How bad is the traffic between here and Dripping Springs?"

"I'd take Congress Avenue south and pick up 290 from there," Sam said. "That way you'll avoid the other roadblocks we have set up."

Eric and Kim walked over with Paco.

"We're in," Eric said. "Dripping Springs RV Park. It's to the north of 290. There's a pretty nasty turn to get in there. After the right turn the access road takes another hard right. Then a tight left, and back about half a mile. Fort Stockton is about four and a half hours from there."

"That's a long drive," Sherry said, looking at Francis.

"We can stop on the way. Ozona or Sonora."

"Don't go to Sonora," Sam said. "Bad attack there a few days ago. The RV Park took the worst of it. Keep your eyes open and your guns handy the whole way."

The caravan was rolling in a matter of minutes, taking the left from the impound yard and heading for Congress Avenue. It was flowing well for near rush-hour, the shadows getting long in the late afternoon.

"You've been to this RV Park?" Kim asked, watching Eric as he drove.

"Yeah," he said. "Never camped there, but one of my buddies lived there for a spell while he was working a construction project. This isn't a recreational park. It's more of a residential place, and like I said, it ain't pretty."

"That's okay," she said. "Think we ought to sprint all the way to Fort Stockton tomorrow?"

"I don't know," he said. "Maybe. That's a long drive, but I'll feel a lot better when we join the others. Might be worth it."

"There's 290," Kim said. "Just up ahead."

"See it," Eric said. he took the right turn, the others following.

"I expected more traffic," Kim said, looking at the long open road ahead of them.

"A lot of the population is hunkering down," Eric said. "Could you imagine being one of the cars at the front of the line earlier? Nowhere to go. They were sitting ducks."

"It's scary to think about," Kim said. "You think the Governor knows what he's doing?"

"Nelson's pretty sharp," Eric said. "So is Chief Ramsey. We could do a lot worse."

"We're getting to the outskirts of town," Kim said. "How much further?"

"We're still in Austin," Eric said. "We have to go past the main part of Dripping Springs. That's where route 12 crosses 290. It's another few miles past there. We've got about twenty minutes to go, give or take."

"Okay," she said. They rode silently for a while, as the houses thinned out. Then there were more houses all of a sudden.

"More people out and about in Dripping Springs," Eric said. "People must feel safer out here."

"I could see that," she said. "It has a small-town feel."

"Shopping center coming up," Eric said. "There's route 12. Won't be long now."

"Good," she said. "I'm tired."

"Me too. Gun battles and interrogations take a lot out of you." He chuckled.

"You think the enemy is really getting the tanks?" Kim asked.

"I'd bet money on it," Eric said. "I hope the National Guard can find them before a bunch of people get killed."

"Now we're out in the middle of nowhere again," Kim said, looking at the rolling hills on either side of the road.

"Texas Hill Country," Eric said. "I didn't want to leave."

"Why did you?"

"Job," he said. "It wasn't a bad move, all in all." He gave her a sidelong glance.

"That's true. You met me."

Eric laughed. "Yeah, you're right. Our road is coming up. I think after this bluff and the curve that follows it."

They climbed the bluff, and suddenly there was a small sign. Dripping Springs RV Park.

"I better slow down," Eric said. He pushed hard on the brakes of the Class C. "Whoa."

"That comes up fast," Kim said as Eric struggled to make the sharp turn.

"Yeah, it does. I almost overshot it." He drove up the incline and made a sharp turn to the left, getting on the small country road.

"I can't even see 290 behind us now," Kim said. "Maybe this is exactly the kind of place we need tonight."

"Hope it hasn't rained lately. This park is all dirt and it gets muddy fast. I almost got stuck back here once, after a poker game. Started raining hard. We waited too long to leave."

"Doesn't look like it's been raining lately," Kim said. "This road dead-ends, see?"

"Yeah, we make a left, then go down a few blocks, then make a right."

"There's a cow in the road up ahead," Kim said, pointing.

"Oh, yeah, forgot about them. They come out of that pasture over there in the morning, and come back in at night. I've had to wait for them before."

Eric drove slowly around the cow. Other cows were heading for the road behind it from the left side of the road.

"Wow, look at all of them," Kim said "There's even some calves."

Paco growled.

"Don't worry, boy, they won't hurt you," Eric said. "There's the park driveway."

Kim giggled as they drove up to the gate. "You weren't kidding about this place. Geez."

An old man wearing a battered cowboy hat trotted up to Eric's window.

"You folks got reservations?" the man asked. He was missing a couple teeth.

"I'm Eric," he said. "Called a while ago."

"Good," the man said. "I'm Jody. We got the space right next to the front building, another one three spaces down from that, and two in the back. Sorry we can't put you guys together."

"No worries," Eric said.

"The gate code is real difficult. 1-2-3-4. It's mainly just to keep the damn cows out of here."

"That's easy, thanks. Need to see my card?"

"No, already charged it. We're cool. Enjoy. Oh, and don't let that little dog roam around after dark by his self. Bobcats and coyotes around here. Pigs too, every once in a while, but they can't get past the fences."

"Thanks," Eric said. He drove up to the gate and punched in the code. The sliding chain-link gate rolled slowly over to the side. Eric saw Jody talking to Dirk as he drove in.

"You paid for them too?"

"Yeah," Eric said. "We'll settle up later."

"Is this place cheap?"

"No, it's kind of expensive for overnighters. Not a bad deal if you're staying a month or more, though."

"I'm surprised," Kim said, watching as Eric pulled over to the side.

"There's a shortage of RV Parks around here," Eric said. He shut off the engine. "Got to un-hitch the Bronco."

"Okay," she said. "I'll come watch. I should know how."

"All right," Eric said. They got out of the car and walked to the back. Dirk pulled up in his pickup and trailer.

"Taking that one, eh?" he asked.

"Yeah. You taking the back?"

"Yeah," Dirk said.

"You got enough sleeping space?" Kim asked.

"Yeah," he said. "The girls sleep in the back of the suburban. The rest of us fit in the trailer, and we still got the back of the truck too. The camper top is pretty well insulated."

"It's not gonna be cold tonight," Eric said.

"Yeah," Dirk said. "Well, I'm gonna go get set up. Why don't you two come over after you're set up. We'll have a beer or two. I got some beef too. I'll cook it up."

Eric looked at Kim, and she shook her head yes. "Fine, we'll be over in a little while."

"There go the cows," Kim said, pointing into the pasture next door. "Now I feel like I'm in Texas."

Dirk chuckled. "See you two later." He drove his rig forward, the suburban following.

Eric and Kim finished with the Bronco. Kim moved it out of the way as Eric jockeyed the Class C and started backing it in. He was almost there when Kim rushed over to guide him the final few feet.

"You're far enough," she called out. Eric shut down, and they did the utilities together, then went into the coach.

"Shall we take Paco out?" Kim asked.

"Sure, might as well," Eric said. They hooked him to the leash and walked along the pasture fence, watching the cows and a few goats meander towards the barn in the distance. The sun was below the horizon. Paco froze and watched a goat and its kid approach. He growled, and the mama goat turned and headed back to the main group of animals. Eric looked at Kim and smiled.

"It's peaceful back here," Kim said.

"Yeah, it is," Eric said.

"Not very nice RVs, though."

"These folks are either working or poor," Eric said quietly. "Or both, I suppose."

"What's it cost to stay here full time?"

"Only $550 per month plus utilities," Eric said. "If you don't have to make payments on your RV, that's a damn cheap way to live."

"You aren't kidding," Kim said. "This is bigger than it looks from the front."

"Yep," Eric said. "They expanded it back further since the last time I was here."

"Looks like Dirk's already set up."

"Yeah. Maybe we should go over there now, instead of taking Paco back first."

"Fine by me, if they don't mind," Kim said.

They walked over. The young girls were sitting in folding chairs next to the Suburban, chatting and giggling. Francis and Sherry were sitting in chairs closer to the trailer. Chance, Dirk, and Don came around the back end of the trailer, carrying a barbecue and a bag of charcoal briquettes.

"Hey, guys," Dirk said, smiling. "Just about ready to break out the beer. Ready for one?"

"Sure," Eric said. "Want us to take Paco back to our rig?"

"Nah, he's welcome here," Dirk said.

"Great, thanks," Eric said.

Dirk headed towards the door of his trailer. After a few seconds, he poked his head out. "You guys better get in here."

"Uh oh," Chance said. "What?"

"North Korea is getting ready to fire off its ICBMs."

"I'll hold onto Paco," Kim said as Eric got up. "I don't want to watch that."

"I'm with you," Sherry said as Francis got up. "Come sit by me and let's get acquainted."

Kim smiled and came over with Paco as the men went inside.

"What's going on?" Alyssa asked. "Why are the men going inside?"

"War news, honey," Sherry said.

"See you in a few minutes, Kim," Eric said. He followed the others into the trailer.

"Got it on CNN," Dirk said. As everybody squeezed inside, he opened the fridge and started handing out beers.

"That rocket is fueling up," Chance said. "How are they getting that video?"

Suddenly there was a bright flash on the screen, and the video feed went dead.

"Yes!" Eric said. "I think we just took out that missile."

"Either that or somebody took out the video camera," Don said.

"Turn it up, man," Chance said.

"You're closer," Dirk said. Chance nodded and turned up the volume.

"Although we don't have confirmation yet, it appears that we have taken out that missile facility. We also have unconfirmed reports that there are other attacks happening against North Korea right now."

"Yaahooo!" Chance yelled.

"Listen," Dirk said. They all shut up, and the sound of others cheering in the park floated around them.

Kim and Sherry poked their heads into the trailer.

"What just happened?" Sherry asked.

"We just took out North Korea's ICBMs," Francis told her.

"Good," Sherry said. "Didn't like the graphics we saw yesterday on their missile range. Not one bit."

"Want to come in and watch?" Dirk asked. "There's room."

"I think I'll sit this out," Sherry said. She looked at Kim. "Go ahead if you want to watch."

"I'll pass," she said.

"Good," Sherry said. "Dirk, honey, pass me that bottle of Southern Comfort I saw in the cupboard earlier, and two glasses."

Dirk chuckled. "Coming right up."

Kim looked at Eric and shrugged. He gave her a thumbs up, and she followed Sherry outside.

"So what now?" Chance asked.

"If we've taken out all of their missiles, we might not have to bomb the hell out of them," Dirk said.

"Yeah, maybe," Don said. "I hope we take out the leadership."

"Don't they have the third of fourth largest army in the world?" Chance asked.

"Yeah," Eric said. "We've got a lot of troops over there, too. I hope they're okay."

"We are getting confirmed reports that the US Air Force has been able to take out all of the missile sites in North Korea. A huge force of North Korean infantry surged across the DMZ. As soon as they reached South Korea, they surrendered. There are reports of North Korean soldiers shooting their officers at that time. The Chinese army is now pushing southward from their border, taking out all North Korean military installations with little or no resistance."

"Good," Eric said.

"Hate to see the Chinese going in there," Chance said. "That's just gonna cause problems later."

"Maybe," Dirk said. "Whose side are the Chinese on now?"

"Their side," Eric said. "As usual. Same with the Russians, I suspect."

"In other news, there has been widespread violence in Great Britain, France, The Netherlands, and Denmark. The Muslim minorities in those countries have come out in force to protest the actions of western countries during this crisis. Angry mobs of natives in those countries have attacked the protesters, and in almost all cases, the local police have been standing aside and letting the violence go on, resulting in injury and death for many of the protesters. In London the police did draw the line when a group of hooligans attempted to go into a Muslim neighborhood and pull people out of their homes."

Chance cracked up. "Soccer hooligans."

"People are finally waking up," Francis said. "Pity it took so much bloodshed."

"I'm surprised the governments are finally doing the right thing," Dirk said. "After all, they caused this mess. They let subversives into our societies in the name of diversity. They called anybody who disagreed a racist. Same with the lackey media."

Chance laughed. "Yeah, in the EU and Canada they jailed people for hate speech when they protested. Our stupid Administration would have done the same thing if not for the First Amendment."

"Okay, I think I'd better go get the coals started," Dirk said.

"I've had enough too," Don said.

"Yeah," Francis said. "I'll sleep better tonight."

"I won't," Chance said. "This fight is only just starting."

{ 9 }

Hospital

Kip Hendrix was back at work in the morning, almost caught up on sleep from the day before. Maria wasn't there yet, much to his disappointment. He turned on the coffee maker and walked into his office, noticing the blinking light on his phone. Coffee first. Jerry Sutton walked into the suite as he was getting to the machine.

"Jerry, how are you?" Hendrix asked.

"You look chipper after such a long day," Sutton said.

"Want a cup of coffee?"

"Sure," he said. "Thanks, boss. Where's Maria?"

"I don't know." Hendrix made two cups, and they walked into the office.

"She was being pretty buddy-buddy with you yesterday in the bunker. Hope you weren't with her last night."

Hendrix smiled at him. "No, I wasn't. I slept. By myself. What's on your mind?"

"There was a big tactical meeting yesterday. Hear about it?"

"I knew it was happening, but I didn't need to be there," Hendrix said. "You know something about it, or are you pumping me for info?"

"You know what it was about?" Sutton asked.

"That massacre at the roadblock yesterday, some missing M-1 Tanks, and some tips about the safety of our dams."

"Dams?" Sutton asked.

"We have reason to believe they're being targeted."

"Oh, okay," Sutton said. "Damn terrorists."

"I didn't tell you what you wanted to hear, did I?" Hendrix asked.

"I heard a really bad rumor," Sutton said.

"Well, out with it."

"The roadblock wasn't just to check out people coming into Austin. There were radiation detectors there. Our intelligence services think a nuclear device could be driven into our cities in a truck."

Hendrix sighed, and reached for his TV remote. He switched it on and turned the sound way up, then gestured to Sutton. They met in front of it.

"The walls might have ears," Hendrix whispered in his ear.

"Shit," Sutton said.

"There was a nuclear device found in a boat off Kemah, just seconds before it was gonna go off."

"My God," Sutton said.

"We've got the harbors locked down now, but the device was small enough to put into a truck. Everybody's going crazy."

"Now the roadblock attack makes more sense," Sutton whispered. "Is that what they think will happen in the lakes?"

"No, that's something else," Hendrix said. "They wouldn't even tell me about that one. I'm lucky to know they're even worried about the dams."

"Geez," Sutton said. "Maybe it's time to take all that built-up vacation."

"Don't you dare," Hendrix said, reaching to shut off the TV. They went back to their seats.

"I was kidding, Kip."

"I know," Hendrix said. "If you think you're the only one scared about this, you'd be wrong."

"Okay, fair enough," Sutton said. "What's Holly think about all this?"

"Haven't talked to him since we got out of the bunker," Hendrix said. "I've got at least one phone message to listen to. Run along and I'll do that."

Sutton stood up. "You'll tell me if you hear anything else?"

"Depends on what it is," Hendrix said, grinning.

"Okay," he said, "and watch yourself with Maria. That display in the bunker yesterday worried me."

"Maybe she's actually interested," Hendrix said. "Fear and stress make some women seek a protector."

"You'd better be sure about that. I'd advise against it even if you are."

"Duly noted," Hendrix said. "See you later."

Sutton left. Hendrix leaned back in his chair a moment, thinking. Then he picked up the phone receiver and hit the message button, playing the first message.

"Kip, it's Holly. You know what this meeting is about? Assholes woke me up. Should I go, or can I blow it off?"

Hendrix deleted the message. "Horse left the barn on that one." He played the next one.

"Mr. Hendrix, this is the Assistant Attorney General. Please call me back. Things have changed. We need to talk. Sorry about last time."

Hendrix chuckled and saved the message. "One more." He played the last one.

"Mr. Hendrix," Maria said, crying. "Celia had a nervous breakdown after seeing all of the nuclear attacks. I don't know what to do. She doesn't have money or insurance, but she needs to go to the hospital. Please call me."

Hendrix hit the callback button. It rang twice, and clicked.

"Maria?" Hendrix asked.

"Oh, thank God," she said. "I don't know what to do. I'm afraid my sister is going to hurt herself."

"Oh no. So sorry. We can get her under observation," Hendrix said. "At least that will keep her from hurting herself in the short term. There's programs that can do follow-up care. I'll help you with that too. So sorry to hear this."

"Thank you, sir," she said. "What do I do?"

"Why don't I come over there? We'll make the arrangements."

"To my place?"

"That's where Celia is, right?"

"Yes," she said. "I don't want to be a bother."

"No bother at all," Hendrix said. "What's your address?"

"You sure?" she asked.

"I'm sure," he said.

"Okay, take I-35 south. Get off on West Slaughter Lane, going west. Then turn left on First Street. I'm in the first big apartment complex on the east side. It's 10100 South First Street. You can't miss it. Second floor, number 202."

"I'll be there shortly," he said. "Don't worry." He ended the call, then rang the switchboard.

"Yes, Mr. Hendrix?"

"Maria is out today, and I have to leave for a while. Please tell whoever calls that I'm out of the office on an emergency."

"Is everything alright, sir?"

"It will be." Hendrix got up and left his office, grabbing his coat on the way. He saw Sutton out in the lobby.

"Going somewhere?" he asked.

"Just a personal issue," he said. "I'll be back later. Call my cell if there's an emergency."

"Okay," Sutton said, eyeing him as he rushed to the parking lot.

The drive to I-35 was stop and go, but once on it, Hendrix moved fast in his Mercedes SUV. "Must be the roadblock up north," he said to himself.

Slaughter Lane was a huge street, bumper to bumper all the way to First Street. He took the left, his heart starting to beat faster. Maria's pretty face and shapely curves filled his mind's eye. He saw the huge park over to his right. Mary Moore Searight Metropolitan Park. All the hours I worked to improve that park, over the objections of the budget cutters. Public opinion helped him to win out. It was one of his first big victories. Not a month went by where he didn't get a nice comment from somebody about his work for that park. Will I blow it now?

The apartment complex loomed to his left. He turned into the parking lot and pulled in near the front, then trotted to the lobby. The elevators were to his right. He punched the button and rode to the second floor and found Maria's unit.

Maria opened the door seconds after he knocked, eyes full of panic.

"Thanks so much for coming," she said. She gave him a quick friend hug and they went inside. Hendrix looked at her eyes, red from crying. She had on a robe and her hair was a mess.

"I don't know what to do," she said, voice trembling.

"Where is she?" he asked.

"She locked herself in the bathroom a while ago. She was crying, but now I can't hear anything. She won't answer me."

"That the door?" he asked, pointing to a door on the left side.

"Yes," she said. "I don't have a key."

Hendrix pounded on the door hard. "Celia, open up. Please."

Nothing.

"I'm gonna have to break down the door," he said.

"Do it," she said, tears streaming down her face.

Hendrix raised his leg and kicked hard on the door, which broke open after the third try. Celia was on the floor, two pill bottles on the counter above her. Hendrix looked at the bottle, then checked Celia's pulse.

"Is she all right?" Maria asked.

"Call 911," Hendrix said. "Hurry."

Maria ran out to the kitchen and got on the phone while Hendrix checked her out. She looked slightly younger than Maria, with a face even prettier, hair in a short black bob. He lifted her and carried her to the couch. Her breath was shallow.

"They're coming," Maria said, still hanging onto the phone receiver. "They want me to stay on the line. Is she breathing?"

"Barely," Hendrix said, concern on her face. "Were those your pills?"

"No, they were hers," Maria said. "She's had problems with panic attacks and depression. I'm so worried about her. She has trouble holding down jobs. I was hoping that Austin would perk her up a little bit."

"Depression can be hard to live with, no matter where you are," Hendrix said.

"You've had problems with that?" she asked. "Oh, sorry, that's none of my business."

"Don't worry about it," Hendrix said. "My mother had problems. She killed herself when I was fourteen."

"Oh my God, I'm so sorry," Maria said, eyes softening as she looked at him. "How did you cope with that?"

"You wouldn't believe it," he said.

Maria put the phone tighter to her ear. "Yes, take the elevator. Go right. I'm only two doors down."

"I'll go open the door," Hendrix said, getting to his feet. He opened it, then heard the ding of the elevator bell. The paramedic team rushed down the hallway with a gurney.

"Kip Hendrix," the first paramedic said. "Nice to meet you, sir. In there?"

"Yes," Hendrix said, holding the door as they pushed the gurney through. "On the couch."

They rushed over, two of the men working her vitals right away. Maria stood behind them watching, her brow furrowed with worry. Hendrix rushed into the bathroom, picked up the two empty bottles, and handed them to the lead paramedic.

"Here's what she took," Hendrix said.

"Thanks," he said, turning and speaking into his radio.

"I hope it's not too late," Maria said, looking up at Hendrix as he stood next to her.

"Me too," Hendrix said.

The lead paramedic pulled Maria aside. "This isn't the most dangerous drug, but we don't have much time. We've got to take her to the hospital now."

"Do it," Maria said. "Can I ride along?"

"No, you'll have to follow. We're going to Saint David's."

"I'll take you," Hendrix said. "You're too worked up to drive."

"You don't have to do that," she said. "You're a busy man."

"It's fine," Hendrix said. "Don't worry about it. Please."

She looked at him for a moment.

"We've got to go," the paramedic said. The men wheeled Celia out the door and down the hall.

"Need to take anything?" Hendrix asked.

"I need to get dressed," she said, glancing at herself in a mirror hanging near the door. "Geez, look at me! I didn't even think."

"I'll wait out in the hall if you'd like," Hendrix said.

"Don't be silly. Have a seat on the couch. I'll be out in a minute." She turned and rushed into her bedroom, shutting the door behind her.

Hendrix sat and pulled his phone out of his pocket to check his emails. Nothing interesting. He was just about to look at the web browser when the bedroom door opened. Maria came out in pants and a pull-over blouse, much more form fitting than he was used to seeing her in at work. It was a struggle for him to keep his eyes on her face.

"You ready?" she asked.

"Yes," he said, getting up. He walked her to the elevator, riding it down to the lobby.

"Wow, those guys are fast," Maria said. "The ambulance is already gone."

"They're professionals," Hendrix said. "There's my car." He clicked the fob and it beeped and unlocked. He pushed another button and the engine started.

"Nice car," she said as they walked up. He opened the passenger door for her, then raced around and got behind the wheel.

"I think we ought to take I-35 to 71," Hendrix said. "Be there in a few minutes."

"That's how I would go," Maria said, watching him. "You really are a nice man, aren't you? Thanks for this."

"I have my moments," Hendrix said as he got onto I-35. They got to the Hospital in no time. He parked in one of the reserved parking places and pulled out a government placard, hanging it on the rear-view mirror.

"What's that?" she asked.

"One of the perks of the job. Most of them are gone now, but we still have this one."

She giggled. "Good."

Hendrix helped her out of the car and they rushed up to the emergency room desk. Maria gave the gray-haired woman her information.

"Here she is," the woman said, looking at the screen of her PC. "They're still working on her. Go have a seat in the waiting area and we'll call you."

"Thank you so much," Maria said. They walked over to an open section of the bench seats against the window.

"Well, we know she got here safe and sound," Hendrix said.

"Yes," Maria said. "You don't have to stick around. I can find a way home."

"I'll wait with you for a while," he said. "Just in case."

"Just in case of what?" Maria asked.

"Just in case there's any insurance or money issues," he said.

"You don't have to…"

"Stop. I'm glad to help. I don't have much in the way of family, and no kids. I'd be happy to help your sister out."

She shot him a wary glance, but then relaxed after a moment. "You're too nice to me," she said softly.

Hendrix just looked at her and smiled. "Want some coffee? You look tired."

"I hardly slept after I got home yesterday," she said.

"You're kidding," Hendrix said. "After we were up all night?"

"Yeah," she said. "Maybe I'll nod off here."

"Go right ahead," Hendrix said. "I'll wake you when they call."

She nodded, fighting it at first, but her eyelids got heavier and heavier. Then she was out, her soft form leaning against Hendrix, snoring softly. He was in bliss.

Two hours later the attendant called Maria's name. Hendrix shook her gently. "Maria, they're calling you."

She woke with a start, sitting up quickly. "I'm so sorry. I hope I didn't drool on you or anything."

"You didn't," he said, smiling at her. "Let's go up there."

The couple went to the desk. "Is she okay?" Maria asked.

"You and your husband can go on back and talk to the doctor," the attendant said. "Right through the door, bed number six."

Maria started to say something, but Hendrix touched her arm and shook his head no. They went through the door.

"Why didn't you want me to say anything?" Maria asked.

"So they wouldn't make me wait outside. You might need me in there. I'll give you privacy if you need it."

"Wonder why she said that? We didn't have rings or anything, and the age difference…"

"I don't know," Hendrix said. "Body language, maybe. You were relaxed with me. You were sleeping against me too, remember? She probably saw that and assumed."

Maria shot him an embarrassed look that turned to a soft smile. It sent a shiver down his spine.

An Asian doctor was standing by the end of the bed talking to a nurse when he saw them walk up. "Are you Maria?" he asked. "I'm Doctor Lee."

"Yes," Maria said.

"And this is?" the Doctor asked.

"Kip," Hendrix said, shaking hands. "How is she?"

"Celia is a very lucky woman," Doctor Lee said. "A couple more hours and she wouldn't have survived."

"Oh my God," Maria said, covering her face, shaking as she began to sob. Hendrix put his arm around her shoulders and pulled her close.

"So what happens now?" Hendrix asked.

"We don't have much choice in the matter at the moment," Doctor Lee said. "She'll be taken to a facility for observation as soon as she's stable enough."

"To make sure she doesn't try it again?" Maria asked.

"Yes," Doctor Lee said.

"For how long?" Maria asked.

"I don't know," he said. "Depends on how the observation goes. Minimally, seventy-two hours, but as a family member, you can work with the facility for more time, which I think she needs."

"Can we talk to her?" Maria asked.

"You're welcome to go behind the curtain, but she'll be unconscious for the better part of a day," Doctor Lee said. "She won't wake up before she's transferred. I'll have the front desk give you a package with the location and contacts for the facility, and some frequently asked questions. Are you her only relative in the area?"

"I'm the only one who's talking to her," Maria said. "Our mother kicked her out because she wouldn't stay med-compliant."

"Okay." Doctor Lee pulled the curtain open. "Go ahead and be with her for a few minutes. Then we've got to get her ready to go."

"Thank you, Doctor Lee," Maria said. Hendrix nodded at him, and he walked to another bed.

"She just looks asleep," Maria said. "I hope she's going to be all right."

"Me too," Hendrix said, looking at Celia's angelic face.

They stayed for a few minutes, and then Doctor Lee came back and walked them to the front desk. The attendant handed her a package with Celia's name on it. Maria smiled and took it. "Thank you."

They walked outside and headed for the Mercedes.

"Thanks so much for taking care of us," Maria said.

"Don't mention it," Hendrix said as he helped her into the passenger seat. "Let's get you home so you can catch up on your sleep."

"I don't know if I can sleep," she said. "I guess I better try. The nap in the waiting room helped."

"Are you hungry? It's almost lunchtime." He looked over at her as he waited for the traffic light to let him drive from the parking lot to the street. She thought about it. The wheels were turning in her brain. He could see that as her brow furrowed.

"Don't you have to get back to work?" she asked.

"The Legislature isn't in session, and I didn't have any meetings today. They know I'm out of the office, and that I'm available by cellphone. It's fine."

She looked at him, locking eyes, searching. Then she sighed. "Okay, that would be nice."

"Great," Hendrix said. "I know just the place." He turned onto the street.

Gun Mount

Kelly was sitting at the dinette in his trailer. It was early morning. His percolator gurgled, filling the coach with the smell of fresh coffee. Brenda walked out of the bedroom.

"Up already?" she asked.

"Couldn't sleep anymore," he said.

"Worried?"

"Yeah," he said. He got up and took two coffee cups out of the cupboard. "Ready?"

"Sure. It's smells heavenly."

"That it does," Kelly said, pouring them each a cup.

"Rachel just climbed out of Junior's rig," Brenda said, looking out the window. "You don't think…"

"Who knows?" Kelly said. "He's always been full of surprises, and we don't know her very well. She might want somebody strong to lean on."

Brenda smiled. "Yes, being with a strong man is a plus in these times. What are you so worried about?"

"Simon Orr," Kelly said.

"Crap, I almost forgot about him," Brenda said. "Heard from that group lately?"

"No," Kelly said. "They ought to be here any time now. I hope nothing went wrong."

"Do they know which park we're in?"

"Yeah," Kelly said. "Jasper was the one who originally told us about this place. He knows Moe pretty well."

"You gonna send them another email?" Brenda asked.

"No," Kelly said. "If they're captured or killed and the enemy has their laptops, I'd be giving them the IP address of this park. Not a good idea."

"Oh," Brenda said. "So we wait."

"And worry," Kelly said.

"Here comes Junior," Brenda said, looking out the window. "He probably smells the coffee."

Kelly smiled and got up to open the door. "Hey, lover boy."

Junior climbed into the coach. "Mind?" He grabbed a coffee cup.

"Help yourself," Kelly said.

"So Rachel's staying at your place, eh?" Brenda asked.

"Of course," Junior said. "Every woman wants a stud."

Kelly laughed. "You haven't laid a hand on her."

"Okay, you found me out," Junior said. "She's more like a kid sister to me, guys. There's no romance going on. She feels safe with me for now, and I enjoy her company. One of the un-attached men in our group will make a play for her soon enough, I suspect. She's a sweetheart."

"You like her, though," Brenda said. "I've seen the way you look at her."

"I love women," Junior said. "Hell, I've looked at you that way before. You're fine, but I never seriously considered trying for you."

"Thank God for small favors," Brenda quipped.

Kelly laughed. "I'm still shocked that I was able to get you."

Brenda laughed. "It was all part of my plan. You men are so clueless."

Kelly and Junior looked at each other and chuckled.

"So what's up today?" Junior asked. He took a sip of his coffee.

"Tank training, apparently," Kelly said. "Ought to be fun."

"They're really going to let us keep those?" Brenda asked.

"For now, according to Jason," Kelly said. "I was talking to him last night. There's some dirty folks at Fort Bliss. The Texas Army National Guard just took over the base and threw a bunch of men in the brig. The Army isn't trustworthy enough to give these tanks back to yet, so they're ours for now."

"Really?" Junior asked. "When did he tell you that?"

"After you hit the sack," Kelly said.

A grinder started up outside.

"What the hell is that?" Brenda asked.

Junior and Kelly rushed to the door and opened it, looking outside. Junior laughed. "Frigging Curt. He's helping Kyle do something to his truck."

"Well, you boys can run along and play with them," Brenda said. "I'm gonna walk over to the showers."

"Just a sec, Junior, I need a warm-up." Kelly poured his cup full. "You need one?"

"Sure," Junior said.

"See you guys later," Brenda said, going into the bedroom as they both left the trailer.

"What the hell are you guys doing?" Junior asked, walking up to Kyle and Curt. Kate sat in a chair, watching.

"They think this is a Mad Max movie," she quipped.

"Damn straight, baby." Kyle grinned in her direction.

"Won't the DPS pull us over if they see a gun mounted on the truck?" she asked.

"We've got connections, remember?" Kyle said.

"The roll bar looks pretty good on here," Curt said, standing back to look. "Looks like a bad-ass off-road truck now."

"It does," Junior said. "I assume you're going to put one of those grenade launchers up there."

"You assume wrong," Curt said. "We're going to put the remote-control .50 cal from that broken tank on there."

"Holy shit," Kelly said.

"Yeah, that's what the enemy is gonna say when we part their hair with this thing," Kyle said.

"You get that roll bar in town?" Kelly asked.

"Yeah," Curt said. "You ought to get one for your pickup."

"I'm thinking about it," he said. "You got any more .50 cals?"

"No, but there are several more Mark 19 Grenade launchers at my place in San Antonio."

"Oh, yeah!" Junior said.

"We have to go get those," Kelly said. "That'll be a dangerous trip."

"It will," Curt said.

"If we have to leave this place, think we'll be taking the tanks?" Junior asked.

"That'll be rough," Curt said. "They fuel like crazy, and they don't use regular gas. If we do want to move them, we'd be better off fixing those flatbeds."

"How much damage is there to them?" Junior asked.

"Tires, mainly. I saw one of them with a shot-up brake line, but I can fix that. The one with the busted tank on it is pretty messed up, but we don't have a way to drive that tank off of there anyway."

"Wonder how much those tires cost?" Junior asked. "They're huge."

"Probably only available through the military," Curt said. "Maybe we could get some help on that."

"Maybe," Kyle said.

"Will those tanks allow us to stay here longer?" Kate asked. "It'd sure be nice to hang out for a while."

"They're a double-edged sword," Kyle said. "They offer some good solid protection, but they might also draw the enemy. If they can take us out, they can have the tanks."

"Wonder what they think about us?" Junior asked.

"Well, we've killed quite a few of their people, so we aren't high on their friendly list," Kelly said.

"That's not what I meant," Junior said. "I know they're mad at us. I wonder if they underestimate us or overestimate us."

"Oh," Kelly said. "That's a good question."

"They didn't know we were here," Curt said. "Pretty obvious to me. They were only here to take the tanks."

"Crap, what about their cell phones?" Junior said.

"I burned them," Curt said. "As soon as you guys left with the tanks. That doesn't mean they don't know the location, of course."

"I wish this park was further out in the boonies," Kyle said.

"This world has gotten too small to hide in the wilderness," Curt said.

Moe and Clancy trotted over to them.

"What's up?" Kyle asked. "You guys look worried."

Moe tried to catch his breath. "I'm too old and fat for all this running around."

"I was up on the roof with the binoculars," Clancy said. "Been watching the road. Saw a couple of trucks stopping by the flatbeds. They're collecting bodies now."

"Crap," Kyle said. "Can they see the tanks over here?"

"Not very well," Curt said. "The one on the top of the bluff was visible from there, but I told Tyler and Logan to pull it down."

"Should we go kill them?" Kelly asked.

"No, let's see if they come looking for us," Curt said.

"You sure you got all their phones?" Kyle asked.

"Yeah, I used my hijacked app to find them. If there were any left, they weren't putting out a signal."

"So they either knew about the location from communication with these guys before we wasted them," Junior said, "or they've got another way to track them."

"That's an unsettling thought," Kate said.

"What do you want to do?" Moe asked.

"Watch what they do and where they go, but don't do anything to give our position away," Curt said.

"Make sure Tyler and Logan know about this in case we have to blast them," Kyle said, "but tell them not to tip them off that we're here. Keep the tanks down unless we know they're coming for us."

"Yeah, that's good advice," Curt said.

"Okay, I'll run over and tell them," Clancy said. He took off, binoculars hanging from his neck.

"What in tarnation are you doing?" Moe asked, looking at Kyle's truck.

"Mounting one of the guns from the busted tank," Curt said.

Moe snickered. "Really, now?"

Brenda walked towards them, hair wet, towel draped over her arms. "Something going on? I saw Moe and Clancy run over here." She saw Moe standing with the others as she got closer. "Oh, you're still here."

"Somebody's picking up bodies from where those flatbeds are," Moe said. "Clancy saw them."

"Dammit," she said. "We gonna do anything?"

"Watch and be ready," Kelly said. "They probably don't know we're here."

"I hope they don't," she said. "I'm gonna go hang up my towels."

"Okay, sweetie," Kelly said.

Junior snickered. "I'm still not used to that."

"Me neither," Curt said. "We can't do anything else on the truck right now. Don't want to run the grinder. It'll make too much noise."

"I figured," Kyle said. "That's okay, I'm ready for a break anyway. Anybody want coffee?"

"I'll take some," Kate said. "C'mon, let's go fire up the machine."

"I've still got some in the back of my toy hauler," Curt said. "See you guys later."

Kyle and Kate went into their trailer.

"Well, guess I'll go back inside too," Kelly said. "Join me if you want, Junior."

"I'm gonna go see what Rachel is up to. Saw her get back to my rig a few minutes ago."

Clancy rushed back over, out of breath.

"Well?" Moe asked.

"They took the bodies and left the way they came."

"East?" Curt asked.

"Yeah," Clancy said.

"They ever look in this direction?" Moe asked.

"Nope, not that I saw," Clancy said.

"That means I can get back to work," Curt said. He picked up his electric grinder and started working on the mounting spot for the gun.

{ 11 }

The Gulf

Juan Carlos, Brendan, and Richardson walked into the bar on a pier off South Padre Island.

"This is cool, dude," Juan Carlos said. "Glad we didn't pull river duty."

"This is gonna be more dangerous," Richardson said. "You know that, right?"

"Yeah, but look at our crib, and it's walking distance from this joint," Juan Carlos said. They walked up the bar and took stools next to each other.

"Yeah, got to admit this place is cool," Brendan said. "Nothing like this along the Rio Grande."

"They saying what caused that dam to break yet?" Juan Carlos asked.

"No," Richardson asked.

"No, they haven't told you, or no, you ain't telling us?" Brendan asked. He looked at Juan Carlos and they both cracked up.

"They haven't told me anything," Richardson said. "I'm done worrying about it. No dams around here."

The bartender was a pretty Hispanic woman, not much older than Juan Carlos and Brendan.

"What's cookin, baby?" Juan Carlos said.

She flashed a smile. "Oh, brother. You guys part of the coast guard?"

"DPS," Richardson said.

"Oh, really," she said, lighting up as she looked at him.

"Looks like she likes older guys," Brendan said. Juan Carlos laughed as the bartender rolled her eyes. "What can I get for you guys?"

"Got IPA on draft?" Richardson asked. "Something local?"

"Of course," she said.

"I'll take that, then," Richardson said. "Give these punks whatever they want. It's on me."

"Punks?" Juan Carlos said. "That's harsh, dude."

"He's showing off his age to the lady," Brendan said. "Nobody says punks anymore."

"What's your name, baby?" Juan Carlos asked.

"Lita," she said.

"Well, Lita, I'll take what the old man is having."

Brendan laughed. "He's gonna want an Ensure after that beer."

"Give it a rest," Richardson said, sheepish grin on his face.

"I don't think he's too old," Lita said, reaching across the bar and giving Richardson a smack on the lips.

"Wow!" Juan Carlos said. "I'm older than I look, you know."

"Oh, you're not seventeen?" She giggled at him. Richardson laughed.

"Okay, all kidding on the side, I'll take the IPA too," Brendan said. "And thanks, Lieutenant."

"Lieutenant, eh?" Lita asked. "Very impressive." She turned and walked away, making sure her hips swayed a little more than usual.

"Damn, she's hot," Juan Carlos said. "And she likes you, boss."

"She's just doing her job," Richardson said. "She is nice to look at, though. That's for damn sure."

"When's the boat gonna get here?" Brendan asked.

"Tomorrow afternoon," he said. "If you want to tie one on, this might be your last chance for a while."

"Hope some more chicks show up," Juan Carlos said.

"Might be kinda dead, with everything going on," Brendan said.

"Maybe, maybe not," Richardson said. "This area is pretty isolated."

"Well, that's the thing," Brendan said. "Lots of hot tourists when it's normal."

Juan Carlos elbowed him, then nodded towards the door.

Brendan looked over and saw two young women walk in, both in short, summery dresses.

"Be still my heart, dude," Juan Carlos said.

"Hey, look," Brendan said. "They know Lita."

They watched as the two women rushed over to Lita, hugging her and giggling.

Richardson chuckled. "Maybe this will be a nice night after all, huh?"

"Hey, they're coming this way," Brendan said, looking scared to death.

"What are you scared of?" Juan Carlos asked. "They're gorgeous."

"Hi, there," the first woman said. She was shapely, with short blonde hair, bright eyes, and dark eyebrows. "I'm Madison."

"I'm Hannah," said the other woman. She was slim with dark brown hair, long and straight. She had vivid dark brown eyes and a warm smile. "I heard you two took out a lot of the invaders at Falcon Lake."

"Yes, that's so cool," Madison said.

"Hey, wait a minute," Brendan said. They looked over at Lita. She was laughing so hard she had to hold onto the bar to keep from falling down.

"You knew Lita before, didn't you dude," Juan Carlos said to Richardson.

Hannah giggled. "They've only been going out for three years."

Richardson chuckled. "Why don't we get a table?"

"You can take that round one by the window, honey," Lita said. "This place is gonna be a ghost town tonight. Everybody split after the bombs went off. I'll be able to hang out with you most of the time."

"Your boss won't mess with you for that?" Juan Carlos asked.

Richardson cracked up.

"Yeah, daddy might mess with me, I suppose," Lita said.

"Oh, that's how it is," Brendan said, laughing. He had a hard time taking his eyes off of Hannah.

"Take a picture, why don't you?" she said, trying to look serious. Her smile broke through.

"You're the most gorgeous woman I've ever seen," Brendan said.

"You've got yourself a romantic," Madison said.

"I can be romantic too," Juan Carlos said. Madison laughed and took his arm as they walked to the table.

"Yeah, I'll bet you can, if we can get past that exterior of yours a little," she said.

Richardson pulled Lita into his arms after she came out from behind the bar. "I'm so glad we got placed here."

"You didn't pull any strings?" she asked, eyes dancing with his. She looked small in his arms.

"No, I didn't pull any strings," Richardson said. "We're liable to be moved around, I'm afraid. Things are crazy right now."

"We'll enjoy it while we can," Lita said. "I had nightmares last night, after you told me about the night the dam broke.

"We were lucky," he said, "and we had Juan Carlos. He's the real hero that night. Got us to safety."

"I'll have to slip that information to Madison," Lita said. "Help me with the beers, okay?"

"Of course," he said. They went back around the bar and drew them, then carried them to the table.

Brendan and Hannah were staring into each other's eyes while Juan Carlos and Madison kept a happy banter going.

"Good lord, look at those two," Lita whispered to Richardson. "That's the way you used to look at me."

"Used to?" he asked.

"Okay, you still do," she said. "I wish you had a different job. You're gone too much, and I miss you so." She started putting beers in front of everybody. Then she and Richardson sat down next to each other.

"So Madison, did Juan Carlos tell you how he saved everybody on the boat when the dam broke?"

"No," Madison said, her eyes bright. "What happened?"

"Nothing much," he said. "I just drove."

Richardson laughed. "That was the best piloting I've ever seen. Brendan and I both owe you our lives."

"Yeah, man," Brendan said.

Juan Carlos got an embarrassed smile on his face. "Well thanks for that. Just doing my job."

"That's what all heroes say," Madison said, brushing his hair off his forehead. She moved in and planted a kiss on him. Richardson and Lita shot each other a glance, and kissed too.

"Let's take a walk on the deck," Hannah said.

"What're you gonna do out there?" Lita asked.

"Make out," Hannah said. Brendan looked like he was going to faint.

"Don't be gone too long," Lita said. "It's been a little dicey out there. Remember last week?"

"We'll stay next to the building," Hannah said, standing and taking Brendan's hands. He followed her in a trance.

"What happened last week?" Richardson asked.

"Somebody took a couple pot shots at the other end of the pier," she said. "They got the guy. He was one of those Venezuelans. A sniper. The cops thought he was trying to terrorize people into leaving the area."

"Shit," Richardson said. "I don't like you being here."

"After they had all the people here searching for bombs, there hasn't been any trouble. I think the bad guys took off."

"I hope so," Richardson said. He looked over at Juan Carlos and Madison. They were still kissing. "Whoa, you two. You only just met."

"Yeah, get a room," Lita said.

"Don't give them ideas like that." Richardson snickered.

"I was just kidding," she said, taking a big drink of her beer.

Juan Carlos and Madison broke their kiss, then looked into each other's eyes.

"Where do you live when we aren't doing this?" Madison asked.

"I grew up in San Antonio," he said.

"You going back there?"

"The way I feel right now, maybe I'll settle wherever you are."

"Oh brother." Madison laughed, then sighed as she looked into his eyes again. "I like you too. We'll see."

Suddenly there was gunfire outside.

"Shit, Brendan!" Juan Carlos said, rushing for the door, Richardson on his heels.

"Get down on the floor, girls!" Richardson yelled as they went outside.

"Oh no," Lita said.

The door flew open and Richardson was back, pushing Brendan and Hannah along. Juan Carlos followed.

"You okay?" Lita asked, rushing over.

"We're fine," Brendan said. "They weren't shooting at us. That was north of here."

"Sounded pretty close to me," Richardson said.

"Let's move away from the windows," Lita said. "There's a little banquet room behind the bar. It's got windows, but they just face another building on the pier."

"Good idea," Juan Carlos said, rushing over to put his arms around Madison and escort her over there.

The others followed, grabbing their beers. Lita turned on the lights.

"Maybe it's not as safe here as we thought," Richardson said to Lita. "Maybe your pop should close down the bar for a little while."

"It'd be closed tonight if not for you guys. I told him I'd open up since I was gonna be here, just in case."

"We should put the closed sign out now," Brendan said.

"Yeah," Richardson said. "The bar is exposed to the windows. It's probably not as bad if you can turn off the lights in the main room."

"Okay," Lita said. "C'mon." She led Richardson out to the door, and flipped the sign to closed, then turned out the lights.

"I like this better anyway," Richardson said, taking her into his arms again. They kissed passionately.

"Hey, what's going on out there?" Juan Carlos said from the banquet room. The others snickered.

"None of your business," Richardson said.

12

Lunch Date

K ip Hendrix drove his sleek Mercedes into the parking lot of the steak house.

"This place is pricey," Maria said.

"That's what expense accounts are for," Hendrix said, smiling as the valet attendant tore a ticket and handed it half of it to him. He got out and rushed around to open the door for Maria.

"Am I dressed well enough for this place?" she asked.

"You look lovely," Hendrix said, taking her hand. "It's fine for lunch. Supper time would require a dress, of course."

They walked into the dark restaurant.

"President Pro Tempore Hendrix," the Maître D' said. "Welcome."

"Thanks, Carl," Hendrix said. "My usual booth open?"

"It is," he said. "Follow me." Hendrix took Maria's arm and they walked into the dark cavernous dining room, to a heavily padded oval booth.

"Wow," Maria said.

"You've never been here before?" Hendrix asked. "On a date or anything?"

"I haven't gone on many dates." She looked uncomfortable.

"Sorry, I didn't mean to pry," he said.

"Drinks?" Carl asked.

"Oh, I suppose we could take the edge off," Hendrix said. "What do you think, Maria?"

"I shouldn't," she said.

"It's okay," Hendrix said. "Whatever you're comfortable with."

She thought about it for a moment. "Oh, why not. I'll take a Bloody Mary."

"Excellent," Carl said, "and for you, sir?"

"My usual," he said. "Martini, up with olives."

"Those are strong," Maria said.

"I'll only have one," Hendrix said. "In case something breaks loose at the office."

"I can go back after this too, if you'd like."

"Nonsense," Hendrix said. "You need to sleep after this. I can't believe you're still awake after last night and the issues with your sister."

"I hope she'll be okay," Maria said. "She's so fragile, and the world is so crazy."

"She had problems before all of this happened, though, didn't she?"

Maria was silent for a moment, looking down. "Yes. She's always had depression, and when the panic attacks started up, it was really hard for her."

"There are medications that can help," Hendrix said.

"I know, but she hasn't always been med-complaint," Maria said. "My mom basically washed her hands of her because of that. I talked her into taking Celia back when she moved here from Zapata, but it only lasted a few days."

"That's hard," Hendrix said. "How about your father?"

"We don't even know where he is," Maria said.

"Sounds a lot like my family," Hendrix said.

"How did you cope with your mom?" Maria looked like she wanted to take it back as soon as it came out. "I'm sorry, I shouldn't ask you about that."

"Don't be silly," he said. "It actually helps to talk about it sometimes, and it was a long, long time ago."

"I don't want to pry," she said. "Tell me to stop if it bothers you, okay?"

"I will," Hendrix said. "My mother had depression and panic attacks too. There were long stretches where she wouldn't leave the house. She'd be med compliant for a while and do fine, but then she'd stop the meds and everything would fall apart."

"Did she try to kill herself before she was successful?" Maria asked.

"Yes," Hendrix said, feeling his eyes tear up.

"Oh, I'm so sorry," she said. "We shouldn't be talking about this."

"No, it's okay," he said. "Really. She had an incident very much like what your sister went through today. I called 9-1-1."

"How old were you?"

"Thirteen," Hendrix said.

"Oh, geez. What did you do when they took her away?"

"I went to live with my grandmother for a while," Hendrix said. "She was a saint. I lived with her after my mother succeeded the following year."

"I'm so sorry you had to live through that," Maria said.

The drinks arrived. Hendrix took a sip of his, watching Maria do the same.

"What were you planning to do with Celia?" Hendrix asked. "After she moved here."

"I don't know," Maria said. She took a bigger sip of her drink. "I was hoping she'd find a job that made her happy. I was hoping I could help her stay on her meds. I was hoping things would go okay between my mother and her, too."

"She's lucky to have a sister like you, Maria," Hendrix said. He took another sip of his Martini, feeling it in his forehead.

"I haven't been a lot of help so far," Maria said.

"Maybe I could find her a job with the state when she gets better," Hendrix said.

"You'd do that?" Maria asked.

"Of course," he said.

Maria was silent for a moment, then looked away. "Is it because you want me?"

"It's because I like you," Hendrix said. "You've told me you don't want an intimate relationship with me. I can take no for an answer."

"But you don't want to," she said.

"I'm fine, really," Hendrix said. "Remember what I said before. I need the company. If I can't be more than a friend, that's just the way it is. To me, it's a whole lot better than nothing."

"It feels like I'm taking advantage," Maria said.

"You aren't," he said.

Carl came over. "Have you decided?"

"Have whatever you want, Maria."

"Thank you," she said. "I'll take the rib eye."

"Very good choice," Carl said. "And you, sir? The usual lunch?"

"Yes, I'll take the Rueben," Hendrix said. "Those are gonna be the death of me yet, Carl. You should be ashamed."

"They are sinfully good, aren't they?" He smiled as he took their menus. "Another drink for either of you?"

"Feel free, Maria," Hendrix said.

"Oh, maybe one more," she said.

"I'd like something a whole lot less powerful," Hendrix said. "Maybe just a single shot of Jameson on the rocks."

"Coming right up," Carl said. He walked away.

"Straight whiskey is less strong than a Martini?" Maria asked.

Hendrix chuckled. "Do you know what's in a Martini?"

"No," she said, a smile slipping on her face as the drink hit her.

"It's two large shots of gin and a little vermouth," Hendrix said. "They're more than twice as strong as a single shot of whiskey."

"Oh," she said. "How about a Bloody Mary?"

"They usually have just one shot of vodka," Hendrix said. "We used those for a hangover remedy when I was in college." He laughed.

"What's so funny?"

"You know who made the best Bloody Mary I've ever had?"

"Who?" she asked, smiling.

"Governor Nelson," he said. "We got drunk together a lot in college. He'd always be the first one up the next morning at the Frat house, mixing Bloody Marys for everybody."

She giggled, her eyes flashing. "You're kidding. He always seems so serious."

"I'll tell you a secret," Hendrix said.

"What?"

"I love that man," Hendrix said. "Like a brother. I'm so glad we're friends again."

"That's so sweet," she said. "I'm happy for you. I wish I had good friends like that."

"Well, you have me," Hendrix said.

"Yes, I do, don't I?" She smiled, then giggled again. "I feel that first drink."

"You don't drink often, do you?"

"No, not very," Maria said. "Oh, here they come."

Carl came over and set their drinks on the table, along with a basket of bread and some whipped butter. "Enjoy," he said as he walked away.

Hendrix took a short sip of his Jameson, watching Maria take a healthy sip of her drink. She's getting a little drunk.

"These are really good," she said.

"Good," Hendrix said. "Mine tastes great too. Not as good as a Martini, but close."

"Maybe I'll try one of those sometime," she said.

"Well, if we go out again, I'll get you one."

"Out? Are we on a date?" She giggled and took another sip.

"Friends can go out on dates," Hendrix said. "Happens all the time."

She took another sip. "I guess so. Hey, can you tell me what you wanted to tell me yesterday?"

He looked around. Nobody was nearby. "We have to get closer. Slide to the middle of the booth and I'll meet you there."

She giggled. "Okay, but watch your hands," she said.

"I've been better, haven't I?" he asked. "I'm not staring at you anymore. I've tried really hard."

"Yes, you have, and I picked this top," she said. "When I noticed it in the mirror on the way out I almost turned around and changed."

"It's lovely," Hendrix said, sliding to the middle. "You did present me with a challenge there, though."

"Sorry," she said. She took another big sip of her drink, a mischievous smile spreading over her face as she slid towards him. "You have been good. I'll tell you what. You can look for a few seconds."

Hendrix smiled. "You don't have to do that."

"Oh, go ahead," she said. "It's my fault. I should have worn something else." She pushed out her chest. "There."

He feasted his eyes, looking at the curve and the hang that he adored, wishing he could touch them, his pulse quickening.

"Time's up." She giggled, but got serious when she looked closely at his face. "Your face is red, and your eyes are..." She looked away. "I'm sorry. That was mean."

Hendrix looked down. "I'm sorry, Maria. I should have refused."

"You've really got a case for me, don't you?" she asked softly.

"Yes, but it's okay," he said. "I can handle it. I'm a grown-up."

"Of course you are," she said. "And so much a better man than I ever imagined." She kissed him lightly on the cheek.

He fought the urge to turn her head to him and kiss her deeply.

"Okay, what were you going to tell me?" she asked.

"It's scary," he said. "You sure you want to know?"

"Yes," she whispered, getting closer.

"You can't tell anybody, no matter what, okay?"

"Okay," she said, her pulse quickening.

He got his face to his ear and whispered. "There was a nuclear device off Kemah. We got to it just seconds before it was going to detonate."

She sucked in air. "Oh my God," she whispered. "What would that have done?"

"Killed a whole lot of people, all the way into Pasadena. Radiation would have covered much of Houston."

"No," she whispered, her breath coming ragged.

"I don't think I should tell you the rest," Hendrix said, backing his head away from her. He missed her scent immediately.

"Why not?" she asked.

"You're so scared," he said. "Your're trembling. Breathing faster."

"It's okay," she said. "Tell me the rest."

"You sure?" he asked, looking at her eyes. They locked, her pulse quickening. Her hand went to his thigh, but then she pulled it away quickly, her eyes dilated.

"Sorry," she said softly.

"I liked it," he said. She shot him an embarrassed glance, and reached for her drink, giving him a chance to check out her lovely form again. She brought the drink to her lips and had another sip.

"I caught you," she whispered, that mischievous smile back on her face. She put her hand back on his thigh again, softly. "Please, tell me."

Hendrix sighed, trying to keep himself under control. *I love this woman.* He got close and whispered again. "That roadblock that got shot up. You heard about that?"

"Yes," she whispered.

"That was there to run radiation sensors on all of the cars coming into Austin from that direction."

Her hand tightened on his thigh, her arm trembling, breath coming faster. "Why?"

"The device they found at Kemah was small enough to put in a vehicle," he whispered.

She squeezed him tighter, then leaned against him, trembling harder. "Oh, God, we could die any minute, couldn't we?"

"That's why I didn't want to tell you," he whispered. "We've got good people looking out for us. Chances are good the enemy won't get anything in here. Trust me."

"I'm so stupid," she said, tears forming around her eyes.

"Why? No you're not."

"I'm worried about slap and tickle in the office when all this is going on," she said.

"Maria," Hendrix said. "I don't have the right to misbehave. You were right to slap me down on that."

Carl came over with their food. "Would you like it there, or where the place settings are?"

"Place settings are fine," Hendrix said, sliding back to his space, feeling Maria's hand slowly come off his thigh. She moved over too, and they ate their meals, being quiet for a little while.

"That was so good," Maria said. "Thanks you."

"You want desert?" he asked.

"No, no, I'm stuffed as it is," she said.

"Okay," Hendrix said.

Carl came back with the check. Hendrix signed and they left, walking into the bright early afternoon. The valet brought the car over and they both got in.

"Are you going to sleep okay tonight, after what I told you?" Hendrix asked as they drove back to her apartment.

"I'll be fine," she said. "It's scary. Puts things into perspective."

"It makes me value my friends more," Hendrix said. "Governor Nelson, and you."

She looked over at him, ready to say something, but she paused.

"You okay?" Hendrix asked.

"I'm glad you're my friend," she said. "Thanks so much for the help with my sister and the lunch."

"You're welcome," he said. He made the turn into her parking lot and pulled into a spot near the door. "Here we are."

She looked at him for a moment. "You want to come in for a little while?"

"I'd love to, but I'll pass," he said. "I'm pretty worked up. I don't want to mess things up."

"You won't," she said.

"I'd feel more comfortable if we didn't push it," he said. "I'd love to take you out again, though. Would you like that?"

"You mean a date?" She giggled.

"A friend date," he said. "What do you think? Tomorrow night, perhaps?"

"Okay," she said.

"Great. Now go get some sleep. I'll see you tomorrow morning."

She bent over to him and kissed his cheek. "Thank you," she whispered.

He looked at her longingly as she hurried to the door of her building.

13

Ranch Road Detour

The sun hit Kim's face through the RV window, waking her.

"Oh, geez," she said, sitting up in bed, holding her head. Eric stirred.

"What's wrong?" he asked.

"Southern Comfort," she said. "My head is killing me."

Eric chuckled. "You were pretty drunk last night. I think Sherry was even worse, though. She was trying to feed the girls some of that stuff before Francis stopped her."

"I remember," Kim said. "I think it scared them."

"They didn't drink any?"

"No," Kim said. "Those are small-town girls."

Eric laughed. "Small town girls were usually more aggressive, at least when I was growing up."

"What do you mean?"

"One of my small-town friends said it best. Nothing for teenagers to do in those little towns except get high and screw."

"Oh, brother," she said, getting out of bed. "Ouch!"

"There's aspirin in the bathroom. Cabinet over the sink."

"I miss anything last night while you guys were inside Dirk's trailer?"

"Not really," Eric said as he got up and went for the coffee maker. "We couldn't decide about today."

"Today?"

"If we should go for broke and drive the five hours to Fort Stockton."

"Oh," she said. "Well, whatever you guys feel comfortable with. I can drive too, you know."

"You ever pulled a trailer?"

"Does a small boat count?"

"Yes," Eric said. "It counts, but they're lighter and easier. It's fine. You should learn. Maybe you should take the first leg today."

"I'm game," she said, "if my head quits banging."

"You'll feel better after some coffee and breakfast," he said. "Trust me. Take a vitamin pill too."

"Does that help?"

"Helps me," Eric said. He brewed a cup of coffee and handed it to her, then made one for himself. "I'm gonna go see what time the others want to leave. Have some cereal."

"Okay, honey," she said, taking a sip of her coffee as he left.

The air was crisp, the cows starting on their daily trip down to the front gate. They might hold us up. Francis was outside the trailer having a smoke. He smiled as Eric walked up.

"Good morning," Francis said. "Sleep okay?"

"Like a baby," Eric said. "Kim didn't feel so good this morning."

Francis snickered. "Neither did Sherry. They drank that whole bottle last night."

"She do that often?"

"Almost never," Francis said. "I'm glad they did last night. Good to blow off a little steam every once in a while. Had to draw the line at the girls joining in, though."

Dirk walked out of the trailer. "Good morning."

"Morning," Eric said. "What time do you guys want to leave?"

"Sooner the better," Dirk said. "You?"

"Same," Eric said. "Want to try for Fort Stockton today?"

"I still think we ought to play that by ear," Dirk said. "Who knows what we'll run into on the road."

"Fair enough," Eric said. "I suggest we keep our weapons handy."

"I agree," Francis said. "Been hearing bad stuff on the grapevine."

"Grapevine?" Eric asked.

"Police message boards, on my laptop earlier," Francis said. "Problems are worse to the east of us, but there have been problems in Sonora, and the southwest part of the state, too. The border with New Mexico is really bad. So is the Rio Grande Valley and along the Gulf."

"We have to drive right by Sonora," Eric said.

Don climbed out of the trailer. "What's up, guys?"

"Just talking about the drive today. We'll try for Fort Stockton, but be ready to stop earlier if we need to."

"Sounds like a plan," he said. "Wish me luck. I'm gonna go wake up the princesses."

Dirk snickered. "Better you than me."

"Gee, thanks for that," Don said as he walked to the Suburban.

"I'll go back to my rig and have breakfast," Eric said. "See you guys in, say, a half hour?"

"Yeah," Dirk said. Francis nodded in agreement.

Eric walked back, listening to teenage girl protests and Don's pleading. He shook his head. *I want to have kids?*

Kim looked a lot better, finishing off her cereal and coffee. "When do they want to leave?"

"Half an hour, give or take," he said, sitting down with a bowl at the dinette. He poured in cereal and milk and started eating.

"I feel a lot better," Kim said. "I think I'll be able to drive."

"Good. Might have to wait a little bit because of our friends out there."

"The cows?" she asked.

"Yeah. Saw them starting towards the road earlier."

"How's Sherry feeling?"

Eric laughed. "About as good as you did when you woke up. Francis said she doesn't drink much."

"Yeah, that's what she told me too," Kim said. "We both needed that."

"You like her?"

"I do," she said. "What is it about drinking that makes you bond so quickly?"

"All your defenses come down," Eric said.

"I'll wash the dishes. Then you can unhook us."

"Okay," Eric said. He finished his cereal and put the bowl in the sink, then got a second cup of coffee. "Don was having fun trying to wake up the girls."

"Yeah, I bet," Kim said.

"You know what ran through my mind?"

"No, what?"

"We want to have some of those?" He laughed.

"I've heard that teenage daughters are a challenge," she said. "Lord knows I was."

"Really?"

"Yes," she said. "My mother and I were in a state of war for much of my adolescence. She had the patience of Job."

"You're a delight," Eric said. "I can't imagine you being that difficult."

"We usually grow out of it," Kim said. "You still want to, though, don't you?"

"Want to what?" he teased.

She came over into his arms and kissed him tenderly. "You still want to put a baby in me?"

"Yes, I do," he said, looking into her eyes as he brushed her hair out of her face. "More than ever."

"Good," she said, turning to get back to the dishes. He slapped her butt. "Hey!"

"Hey, what?" he asked.

"Men," she said. "I'm done with the water."

"I'll go get busy." He left the coach, got into the Bronco, and backed it into position to hitch up. Then he went to the utilities and unhooked them.

"I've got everything stowed, honey," Kim said out the door. Eric got into the driver's seat and looked back at her. "I'm going to pull out. Want to take Paco for a walk?"

"Sure, I'll do that now," she said. Eric watched as she left the coach, and then fired up the engine and pulled forward, turning onto the road and backing towards the Bronco. Dirk was just pulling up behind him as he was hitching her up.

"Paco is done," Kim said as they approached. "I'll get him fed."

"Thanks," he said.

"Ready?" Dirk asked.

"Yep, off we go," Eric said. "We can stay on 290 until it runs into I-10."

"Okay," Dirk said. "Need gas pretty soon?"

"I can make it to Johnson City. You?"

"We can make it that far," Dirk said. "See you there."

Eric got into the coach. Kim was already behind the wheel, adjusting the mirrors. "Anything I need to know that's different than towing a boat?"

"The towing part isn't much different, but driving the coach is. Your back end swings wider, because of the overhang over the back wheels and how close you're sitting to the front wheels. So in turns, especially right turns, don't turn the wheel until you're past the corner. Swing wider than you would in a car."

"Okay," she said. "Here we go." She put the class C into gear and drove forward, the tow-bar doing its initial clunk as the telescoping unit locked in. "Do I need to input the code at the gate?"

"No, there's a metal detector on the inside. It'll open automatically from this side. Watch for cows!"

She giggled. They got through the gate and onto the road, making a left. The cows had already passed.

"This right turn is a little tight," Eric said. "Remember what I said."

She nodded, hands firmly gripping the wheel, taking the turn perfectly.

"Great job," Eric said. "One thing I forgot to mention. Other vehicles going by, especially truck, will rock this puppy quite a bit. Just hold onto the wheel and try to keep her straight. You'll be fine."

"Okay." They rolled down the small country road and made the right turn to the access road, stopping at 290. The highway was empty. Kim drove onto it, hitting the accelerator hard. "Takes a while to get up to speed, doesn't it?"

"Yeah, this engine is working pretty hard, especially when we're towing," Eric said. "It's strong, though. Rebuilt a couple years ago. She's got some guts."

They got to Johnson City, where they stopped to gas up. Kim took Paco out while Eric went to the gas pump. Dirk pulled into the island next to his and started pumping gas.

"Something doesn't feel right here," Eric said, looking around. "Not enough people out and about for this time of morning."

"I was thinking the same thing," Dirk said.

"Where's the Suburban?"

Dirk pointed behind him. "Last island, over there."

"Hope they're keeping the girls out of sight," Eric said.

Dirk looked over at the Suburban. "Shit, I didn't even think about that. Be right back." He trotted over and talked to Don, then hurried back.

"Too late, they already hit the store," Dirk said. "Where's Kim?"

"She's right there," Eric said, pointing to the grass median by the road. "Looks like she's coming back. Maybe I should send her into the store looking for the girls."

Kim came back over and noticed Eric's expression right away. "What's wrong?"

"The girls went into the store by themselves," Eric said. "It's making us nervous. This place doesn't feel right."

"Seems like not enough traffic," Kim said. "It always this dead around here?"

"Not the times I've been here," Eric said, eyes darting around nervously.

"Look, here they come," Kim said, pointing at the store. The girls were walking back to the car with big drinks in their hands, happily chatting.

"Well, they don't seem too nervous," Dirk said.

"No, but look at those guys next to the door of the market," Eric said, nodding.

Kim glanced over at them. "They just look like kids," she said. "They're gonna stare at the girls. They're about the same age."

"You're probably right," Eric said. He finished pumping gas. "The sooner we get out of here, the better."

"Yeah, I think you're right about that," Dirk said. "I keep feeling like we're being watched."

"You two are making me really nervous," Kim said.

"You gonna use the bathroom?" Eric asked.

"In the coach," she said. "I'm not going in the store. You want me to keep driving?"

"Yeah," Eric said. "I'm going to bring one of the AKs up to the front."

Dirk nodded at him as he put the gas pump nozzle back. "I'll do the same. Keep your eyes open."

"Will do," Eric said. He got back inside the coach just as Kim was climbing into the driver's seat.

"Ready to go?" she asked.

"Yeah. I'll be up there in a second."

"All right, sweetie." She drove off the gas station lot and headed back towards 290, Don's Suburban and Dirk's pickup and trailer following.

"Good, Don's in the middle now," Eric said, sitting in the passenger seat and putting the AK next to him on the floor. "That's better. He's by himself with the girls. They ought to have somebody riding shotgun."

"Yeah, I'm surprised Chance or Francis didn't ride with them," Kim said.

The caravan got to 290 and sped up, Eric checking the rear-view mirror every minute or two and scanning the sides and front.

"You really look nervous," Kim said. "Did you actually see somebody watching us, or is it just a feeling?"

"Just a feeling," he said. "Probably nothing. It's been a long few days."

"Yes it has," Kim said. "What's the next town?"

Eric looked at his phone. "Stonewall is only about fifteen minutes away."

"You ever been there?"

"Just passing through," Eric said. "It's pretty small. I'd say under five hundred people."

"You're worried about the girls," Kim said.

"And you," Eric said.

"Why?"

"Because of what we heard at the police station," Eric said.

"We haven't had a situation like this in America for a long time," Kim said.

"Civil War was the last time," Eric said, "other than the Indian wars, and none of those lasted very long."

"How do you think the population is gonna take it?"

"We've already seen some of it," Eric said. "We'll fight to protect our families and our home."

There was a boom in the distance. Kim shot a worried glance at Eric. "What was that?"

"Reminds me of what we heard before we left Carthage," Eric said. "There's another one."

Eric's phone rang. He answered it.

"Eric, you hearing that?" Dirk asked.

"Yeah," he said. "Artillery?"

"Sounds smaller than what they shot Carthage up with, but sounds can be deceptive. What town is coming up?"

"Stonewall. Wonder if that's where it's coming from?" Eric asked.

"There's another one. Louder than before. Wonder if we'll be able to go through the town?"

"We'll find out in about five minutes," Eric said. "We're almost there."

There were two more loud booms, and black smoke was rising down the road ahead.

"Does frigging 290 run right through the middle of Stonewall?" Dirk asked.

"Yeah," Eric said. "Those are Tanks. More than one. You hear how close together those last two shots were?"

"Yeah," Dirk said. "Find us a detour."

"Will do," he said. "Talk to you in a few minutes. Call Don and let him know what's going on."

Okay, man," Dirk said. Eric ended the call and went frantically to his map app.

"We going around the town?" Kim asked.

"Yeah," Eric said. "There's only one choice that I see. Make a left on Ranch Road 1623. It's small, so we'll have to slow way down. Then we can cut back over to 290 on Upper Albert Road."

"How far is it to 1623?"

"About two minutes, so be ready."

"Shit, is that a tank?" she asked, pointing in the distance. Just then the main gun fired, and a structure exploded.

"Son of a bitch," Eric said. "I hope they don't chase us." He hit Dirk's contact.

"Left on Ranch Road 1623. We'll take that down to Upper Albert Road, then get back on 290, if they don't see us."

"Can they catch us on the back roads?" Dirk asked.

"An M-1 Tank will go at least forty-five, and the big gun has some reach, but they look pretty busy," Eric said. "Still, we'll be lucky to get past this. Stay sharp. Watch for smaller vehicles chasing us."

"I'm making the turn," Kim said.

"Gotta go," Eric said. He ended the call. "Good, the tanks probably won't notice us. Look at the trees. Windbreaks almost all the way south."

"Good, that makes me feel better," she said. They sped up on the small country road, brush and trees on either side of the road. Two more booms floated towards them.

"Dammit," Eric said. "I'm calling Sam O'Reilly." He hit the contact. It rang a few times, then clicked.

"Eric?" Sam asked. "Something wrong?"

"Tanks are attacking Stonewall. We just had to take a detour."

"Oh, shit," he said. "They see you?"

"I don't think so," Eric said. "We took a Ranch Road south, and we'll cut over to 290 south of the town. Other people are gonna run right into the middle of this, though. You know 290 runs right through the middle of the town, right?"

"Yeah, I've been there many times. I'll make some calls. Thanks for telling me. How many tanks?"

"At least two, judging by the rate of cannon fire," Eric said.

"Okay, talk to you later. Be careful."

Eric ended the call. "Hopefully there's enough of the Texas Air National Guard left to do something."

"Won't that kill a lot of people in town?"

"Most of them are probably already dead," Eric said.

"How much further on this road?"

Eric looked at his phone. "Couple miles."

"We're losing our cover," she said.

"It's okay, we're far enough away now. If the tanks saw us and cared, they'd already be lobbing shells over here."

"Could they hit us?"

"Distance-wise, probably, but they can't get a clear shot through the trees and brush."

Eric's phone rang again. "Dirk," he said, putting it to his hear.

"Hey, man, you call this in?" Dirk asked.

"Yeah, just called Sam O'Reilly."

"Good," he said. "We coming up to that second road?"

"Any minute now. Watch for smaller vehicles coming after us. If we're gonna get hit, that's how it'll happen. You got our back door."

"Roger that," he said. "Later."

Eric ended the call. "There's the road. Tight right turn."

"See it," Kim said, slowing down. She took the turn onto the small road. "Shit, this is only one lane."

"Yeah, I figured," Eric said. "Hear that?"

"What is that?" Kim asked, eyes wide. Eric smiled back at her.

"Jets," he said. "Probably the Texas Air National Guard."

Suddenly there were explosions to the north.

"Those poor people," Kim said as she struggled to keep the rig on the thin, broken asphalt.

"Fireballs," Eric said, looking out his window. "Wow."

There was silence after a few more explosions. Eric started to settle down. The road got tighter, branches scraping the roof of the coach from time to time.

"We doing damage?" Kim asked.

"I'll have to look at the roof. Might have to patch the rubber."

"Is that a big deal?"

"Nah," he said. "Had to do it before."

"How much further to 290?"

Eric looked at his phone again, moving his finger across the surface. "It'll take a while. There's a left curve coming up, and then a little further there's a sharp right, which will take us towards the north again."

"Hope nobody comes the other direction," Kim said.

"Most of the people who would be back here probably have four-wheel drive," Eric said. "Don't get off the road."

"Okay," she said.

They made it back to 290 in about twenty minutes. The road was deserted as Kim made the left turn. She gasped as she looked in the rear-view mirror.

"That town is gone," she said.

Jets buzzed them, firing machine guns in back of them as they moved on the road.

"They don't want us on 290," Eric said. "Turn around. We're taking the back roads.

Kim nodded and made a wide turn, heading south again. "We're going to end up on dirt again, aren't we?"

"We might."

14

Juarez

Chief Ramsey rushed into Governor Nelson's office.

"I heard," Nelson said, not even looking up from the papers on his desk.

"Stonewall?" Ramsey asked.

"Yeah, Landry called me," he said. "Who told you?"

"Eric Finley called Sam," Ramsey said as he sat down.

"That boy has been pretty damn helpful," Nelson said.

"He has," Ramsey said. "What did Landry have to say?"

"Three tanks," Nelson said. "The people in them barely knew what they were doing, but that didn't stop them from blowing up several buildings and spewing machine gun fire all over the place. Some of Gallagher's people are going in there to see how many casualties there were."

"There's been medical people there already, though, I hope?"

"Oh, yeah," Nelson said, "almost forty wounded. They're receiving care now. Some of them aren't going to make it."

"Geez," Ramsey said. "I'm thinking that these tanks aren't being moved very far after they're highjacked. Probably why we haven't found them in the east like we expected."

"That's what the real take-away is in this," Nelson said. "These three were highjacked very close to where they attacked. Landry's jets found the flatbed trucks, amongst the hills north of town."

"Dammit," Ramsey said. "We don't know where the highjackings took place."

"I know," Nelson said. "Believe it or not, we've got bigger problems."

"Uh oh," Ramsey said. "What?"

"The enemy has been flooding into New Mexico, and they're massing along our western border. They've already been staging raids into El Paso. Large raids. More than the local PD can handle."

"Damn purple-state New Mexico," Ramsey muttered. "Open border fools."

"Yeah, pretty much," Nelson said, leaning back in his chair. "We'll have to help them to protect ourselves."

"What does that mean?" Ramsey asked.

"It means we'll need to move a significant portion of our National Guard over there to stop the invasion, and then we'll need to pursue the enemy across the border and wipe them out."

"Meanwhile our cities are open to attack," Ramsey said.

"Nobody said this job was gonna be easy," Nelson said. "If we don't shut down that situation, the cities will be even worse off."

Ramsey sighed. "So what do we do?"

"We follow the advice we got from those two generals we talked to a couple days ago," Nelson said.

"Walker and Hogan," Ramsey said.

"Right. We bring in citizens. We have no choice. Here's where the gun laws of Texas will pay off."

Ramsey sat thinking for a moment. "I think I finally got something through my thick skull. Just now."

"What's that?" Nelson asked.

"The reason for taking Texas out of the union," Ramsey said. "They're starting to disarm citizens in the blue states."

"And in the purple states, too, but it's not going well for them. These people are beyond stupid. They can only get away with that in places like Manhattan, Baltimore, Newark, or Chicago. There was a real bloodbath in upstate-New York a couple days ago. Local citizens and law enforcement killed a group of Federal agents who came in to confiscate weapons, after the President extended martial law north of the city."

"Never let a good crisis go to waste," Ramsey said. "Idiots. And the President said he wouldn't do that in his speech, remember? They doing anything about the uprising?"

"Yeah, enforcing a press blackout," Nelson said. "They don't have anywhere near the amount of soldiers needed to put down a rebellion of the size they have building in the rural areas of the New England states."

"So that means they probably wouldn't have tried that in Texas," Ramsey said.

"That made my decision difficult," Nelson said. "Came down to focus."

"Focus?"

"Yeah, I want our citizens to focus on the enemy, not on the Feds. The problem with the Feds will solve itself. The citizens will see to that eventually. They'll take about so much, then they'll be done. Even in the blue states."

"Think so, huh?" Ramsey asked. "Hope you're right. We've been shellacked in the last few national elections."

"I'm watching California carefully right now. It's a blue state because of illegal immigration and the fact that it's been a magnet for lefties for so many years. Conservatives and moderates have lost their voice in government due to that and very shrewd gerrymandering, but look at the initiatives which have passed by landslides. Some of them would have a tough time passing in Texas."

"Haven't paid much attention to the land of fruits and nuts," Ramsey said. "So what about the rest of the tanks?"

"Landry is going to fly reconnaissance missions along I-10, east from Fort Bliss. He'll follow the tributary roads too, like 290 and 62, and I-20. Ought to be able to find them."

"Well, make sure they ignore the ones in Fort Stockton," Ramsey said.

"Don't worry, he knows about those," Nelson said.

"Any news about the other thing?" Ramsey asked.

"What other thing?"

"Kip Hendrix," Ramsey said.

"Oh, that," Nelson said. "Ought to be interesting. They've already approached him, but they're making like they want help with the nuclear attacks and the anti-submarine weapons. We traded some intelligence with them along the back channel already. I told Hendrix it's fine for him to become part of the back channel, but to keep his eyes and ears open and report anything dicey right away."

"You really trust that guy, don't you?"

"Well, yes and no," Nelson said. "I still consider him to be my friend, and I think he loves Texas."

"I'm skeptical," Ramsey said.

"You been keeping an eye on him?"

"Yeah. He spent a good part of the day with his secretary yesterday."

"She his type?"

"In spades," Ramsey said. "Name's Maria. Beautiful Latina. He's being careful, though. Her sister attempted suicide, so Hendrix went over to help. Took Maria to the hospital, then to lunch afterwards."

"What happened to the sister?"

"Under observation for now," Ramsey said. "She's got a history. Poor girl is pretty messed up."

"What happened after lunch?"

"He took her back to her apartment and dropped her off. We expected him to go inside."

"I don't want you to jump to conclusions," Nelson said. "Really. Hendrix has used women in the past more than once, but he's also been a good actor with more than one of them. You know his mom killed herself when he was in his early teens, right?"

"No, I didn't know that," Ramsey said. "We were never that close. I wasn't in his social class, remember?"

Nelson chuckled. "He can be a little elitist. I used to ride him on that all the time. Became kind of a joke, actually."

"Not funny to me," Ramsey said. "So you want me to keep following him?"

"At a distance," Nelson said. "I don't care about what he does with the girl. They might develop real feelings for each other. Not our business. I know office romance can backfire, but look at the times we're in."

"So who do you want me to watch for?"

"Anybody who looks like they might be the enemy, from the local Mosques and such," Nelson said. "Also late night meetings with Holly or his minion."

"Jerry Sutton?"

"Yeah," Nelson said. "Don't get caught. I don't want him to think he has a reason to do something bad. Comprende?"

"Yeah, okay," Ramsey said. "I get it."

"Good," Nelson said. "I'll let you know as soon as I hear anything about Landry's search."

"Thanks," Ramsey said. He got up and left the office.

{ 15 }

Genetics

Jason walked out into the mid-day heat, following the ratchet noise.

"Damn, you're almost done already?" Jason asked, watching as Curt and Kyle torqued the .50 cal and remote control assembly onto the truck's roll bar.

"Hey, brother," Kyle said. "We're making progress."

"How heavy is that?" Jason asked.

"Let's just say it's good that he's got a three-quarter ton pickup with some extra suspension pieces," Curt said.

"You could have put the smaller machine gun on there," Jason said.

"Nah, that ought to go on a lighter vehicle. You know, like a Jeep."

Jason cracked up. "I thought I was getting an M-19."

"We'll see," Curt said. "You probably still will, assuming we can get to San Antonio and back without getting ourselves killed."

"Lovely thought," Carrie said as she walked up.

"Seriously," Kate added.

"I actually have another idea for the 7.62," Curt said, "and we already have a potent off-roader."

"Which we could tow to make it more highway-worthy," Kyle said. "That worked really well. Best of both worlds."

"That's a good point," Curt said.

"So what's the idea?" Jason asked.

"I'm still thinking about it," he said. "I'd need a better video camera than I have in order to pull it off. Might have to go into town and see what they've got."

"Fort Stockton?" Jason said. "Good luck."

"You still haven't told us the idea," Kyle said.

"One crazy idea at a time," Curt said. "Now comes the hard part for this job. Mounting the control. I've got to design something that my 3D printer can handle. I'll talk to you guys later." He jumped out of the pickup truck bed and trotted to the toy hauler, climbing into the garage.

"Should I go help him?" Kyle asked.

"Nah, he has to think," Jason said.

"We just saw something disturbing on the TV in the clubhouse," Kate said.

"Uh oh," Kyle said. "What?"

"Three of these tanks drove into Stonewall and made a big mess. Killed a bunch of people."

"Stonewall?" Kyle asked. "Shit, that's on 290. Hope Eric didn't get caught up in that. He planned to go through there."

"What happened to the tanks?" Jason asked. "They still on the loose?"

"No, they were taken out by some Texas Air National Guard jets," Carrie said.

"Good," Jason said. "I hope they know not to hit ours."

"I was thinking the same thing," Carrie said.

"Maybe we should go get our training done with the tanks," Kyle said.

"I wouldn't bother," Kate said. "They already got enough men trained for all of them. I overheard Logan and Tyler talking to Nate,

Fritz, and Gray about that. They've moved their focus onto those flatbeds. They're trying to find a source for new tires."

"Good," Jason said. "Chances are we won't be able to stay here for long."

"Even with those tanks protecting us?" Carrie asked.

"Yeah, those things ought to help us quite a bit," Kate said.

"There's half a million of these creeps wandering around Texas," Jason said. "We could get hit with a large scale attack, and the tanks would only slow them down."

"Not to mention the fact that there were so many tanks hijacked," Kyle said. "They might attack our tanks with some of their own. They might outnumber us by quite a few tanks, too."

"So what do we do?" Kate asked.

"Watch, wait, strengthen ourselves," Jason said. "Get ready to go on the offensive."

Carrie looked at him, eyes getting glassy. "We have Chelsea to worry about."

"I know, sweetheart, but if we don't win this war, what's her life going to be like?"

"I'm with Carrie," Kate said. "I wish we could just go hide out somewhere."

"There's no place to hide," Kyle said softly, getting closer to her.

"This just figures," Kate said to herself, shaking her head as she went into Kyle's arms.

"What?" Kyle asked.

"I finally find the right person, and it's in the middle of all of this crap," she said.

"I know," Kyle said. "Our timing could have been better."

"You two might never have met if not for this stuff," Carrie said. "Hell, Kate, you didn't exactly want to tag along with us at first, either. Remember?"

Kate giggled. "Yeah, I know. I thought this guy was an over-grown twelve-year-old at first."

"Hey!" Kyle said.

"Oh, don't worry," she said. "You've won me over and then some. I'm yours, gladly. But Carrie is right about the timing."

"Daddy," Chelsea called from the motor home.

"She's awake," Jason said, smiling. "Coming, sweetie. Hungry?"

"Yes," she said. "Can I have a popsicle?"

"I think lunch would be a better idea," Carrie said. "I'll come make you something."

"No, it'll be yucky," Chelsea said, stomping her feet.

"See what you two have to look forward to?" Jason grinned and followed Carrie to the motor home, Kate and Kyle watching. Kate looked up and kissed Kyle passionately.

"Wow," he said. "Middle of the day, huh?"

"I don't understand the feelings I'm having," she said. "It's crazy, but I want that. Now."

"What's that?"

"Children," she said. "I know, stupid idea."

"It's not stupid at all, except for the timing," Kyle said.

"Carrie's pregnant," she said softly.

"Yeah, and Jason is worried sick about it," Kyle said. "The baby is gonna come before this war is over."

"You really think it's gonna be that many months?"

"Yes," Kyle said. He looked her in the eyes. "Shit, you don't care, do you?"

"No, not really," she said. "The urge is too strong. That's what I don't understand. I should be scared of being pregnant in this world, but I'm not. The way I look at it, better to bet on a positive future than to accept a horrible one."

Kyle chuckled. "This isn't unusual, actually. Read an article on that once. Scientific American. The article was mainly about how more boys than girls are born during and right after wars but it also talked about increased fertility in general. Can't remember exactly why. Something to do with genetics."

"Maybe human population is like one big organism," Kate said. "What happens to the group affects individuals beyond what we're conscious of."

"Where we going with this?" Kyle asked.

They locked eyes again, Kyle drawing her tight into his arms. Kate stretched herself up and kissed him again, then backed off and studied his face.

"Out with it," Kyle said softly.

She sighed. "I'm almost out of birth control pills. If I'm going to stay on them, I need to get with my doctor and have the prescription sent to a town around here."

"You don't want to," Kyle said.

"No, I don't, but it's not just my decision."

Kyle was silent for a moment. "You're right, it's not just your decision."

She looked at him. "So what do you want?" she asked, her voice tremoring.

"Don't call your doctor," he said, pulling her close again. "Toss what you have left."

"Oh, God," she said, kissing him again. Then she took his hand and pulled him towards their trailer.

{ 16 }

Cruising the Bay

It was still early, but the sun was bright, Black Skimmers swirling over the water looking for some breakfast to scoop up with their red and black bills.

"There's our baby," Juan Carlos said, walking on the dock with Brendan. "None the worse for wear." There was a tech working on something in the pilot structure.

"It's the only boat here," Brendan said. "I thought Jefferson's boat was gonna be with us."

"Somebody told you that, dude?"

"Nah, I just assumed." Brendan snickered. "You know what they say about that."

"When's Richardson going to be here?"

"Should be any minute," Brendan said. "Probably still playing kissy-kissy with Lita."

"Wish I was still playing kissy-kissy with Madison," Juan Carlos said. "What a dish."

"Think they're going to keep us around here for a while?"

"I hope so," Juan Carlos said. "We'll see. Here comes Richardson.'

"Get any sleep last night?" he asked as he walked up.

"Maybe we should ask you the same question," Brendan asked.

"Yeah, maybe you should," he said as he stood next to them, looking at the boat. "She ready, Cooper?"

The tech looked up at them. "Yeah, Richardson, she's ready. Try not to screw her up."

"How crazy has it been around here?" Brendan asked.

"We've had some sniper activity, but only at night," Cooper said, standing up and climbing onto the dock. He was a tall man with dark hair and a droopy mustache, rubbing his hands on a towel. "Better be careful with that M-19 around here. You hit one of these buildings and there'll be hell to pay."

"Damn, he's right about that," Juan Carlos said. "This is not like the lake."

"No, it's not, and we've got to watch the .50 cal fire too," Richardson said. "Hopefully this will be more patrol and less battle."

"What's our main objective?" Brendan asked.

"Stop incoming boats," Richardson said. "Look for weapons, hidden people,"

"Nuclear bombs," Juan Carlos said, cutting in. Cooper laughed.

"Funny ha ha," Richardson said. "I don't think we'll find any of those, but this is serious business. The danger here is going to be closer in. We have to stay sharp. Especially if we have to board boats."

"Well, that is what we were originally trained for," Juan Carlos said. "All this naval warfare crap came along later, and we never got any training for that."

"Yes we did," Brendan said. "The M-19 training."

"Oh, that's right," Juan Carlos said. "Our SMAW is still under the seat, right?"

"You mean that little bazooka?" Cooper asked. "Yeah, it's still there. Not sure why."

"Do we really need the M-19 in here?" Juan Carlos asked. "Given the risks of grenades flying around populated areas?"

"Yes, for fleeing boats," Richardson said. "Remember the directive that Nelson sent through our high command. Pleasure boating is illegal for the time being. No fisherman, no sight-seers, nothing. Whoever we stop had better have a pretty good reason to be there. If they refuse to stop, we sink them. No quarter."

"So we need to assume that anybody we see is up to no good," Brendan said. "Got it. What happens if we have to escort somebody in? We're the only boat here that I can see."

"There are several more north of here," Richardson said. "We call in any escorts, and we'll get called if we need to move elsewhere to help. We are razor thin, though. Our backstop is air support. Choppers. We have three in the area, ready to take off in a split second."

"We ready to go?" Juan Carlos asked, standing next to the pilot station.

"Yeah, it's time," Richardson said. "We stay out until 2:00 AM, and then the choppers with their night vision take over."

"I'll load the guns," Brendan said, leaping into the boat. Cooper and Richardson untied the lines, then Richardson jumped on.

"Be careful out there," Cooper said. "We've lost people."

"Will do," Richardson said. "Go ahead, Juan Carlos."

He fired up the engines and backed out of the slip.

They cruised slowly out into the bay.

"There isn't an opening to the Gulf nearby, is there?" Brendan asked. He finished loading the .50 cals and moved to the M-19.

"Doesn't look like it, dude," Juan Carlos said. "How far away are the other patrol boats?"

"One's based out of Port Mansfield," Richardson said. "the other one is way up in Baffin Bay."

"Is that far away?" Juan Carlos asked.

"Yeah. There are more boats up further, but they've been stationed here for a while. They aren't transplants from the Rio Grande like we are. They're around Corpus Christi and beyond."

"They don't really expect us to escort anybody, do they?" Brendan said.

"No, if we see unauthorized boats in here, we blast them. Didn't need to tell that contractor about it."

"Anybody check that guy out?" Juan Carlos asked. "He seemed a little sketchy to me."

"Cooper?" Richardson asked. "Yeah, he's okay. Been in the business a long time."

"Watch your speed close to shore," Brendan said. "It's really shallow. I can see the bottom in the dusk, but once it gets dark, it'll be tough."

"We running spotlights?" Juan Carlos asked.

"Yeah, here we run the lights," Richardson said.

"Is there a navigable passage to the Gulf anywhere around here?" Juan Carlos asked. "Looks like a pretty solid coast along here so far."

"Yeah, just south of where the bar was," Richardson said. "Didn't you guys study the charts?"

"We never got any charts."

"Dammit, somebody screwed up there," Richardson said, shaking his head. He pulled out his phone and moved over next to Juan Carlos. "Here's where we were with the girls last night. Right where route 100 crosses the bay on that big bridge. See?"

"Yeah," Juan Carlos said. "That's a huge opening."

"We have Coast Guard gun boats watching that entrance, so we really don't expect anything getting in from the Gulf there, but look southwest, here. That's the border with Mexico. See that long channel?"

"Yeah."

"That's a place to look out for. There's also thousands of boats in and around Port Isabel here. They've been searched, but it wouldn't be that hard to carry something onto them from the docks."

"Geez," Juan Carlos said. "Three boats aren't enough."

"That's why this is dangerous," Richardson said. "We've got new boats on the way, but not overnight."

"They going to build more?" Brendan asked. "Doesn't that take a long time?"

"They aren't building them from scratch," Richardson said. "They're taking some off the private boat production line and retrofitting them with what we need. Armor and the guns and the rest of it. We'll get another eight out of the factory early next week. Four will come here, four to the Rio Grande."

"Where we getting the crews?" Brendan asked.

"Mixture of places," Richardson said. "Coast guard academy. DPS training program. US Navy."

"Good," Juan Carlos said. "Where we going?"

"Let's go to that channel I pointed out. Go all the way back. It's narrow, so we'll need to watch out for snipers on the coast. Then let's go north along the mainland side, cross over and come down the South Padre Island side. Okay?"

"Got it," Juan Carlos said. "Why don't we mount GPS units on here?"

"That was discussed," Richardson said. "They decided against it."

"Cost?" Brendan asked.

"No, they want everybody to be trained in how to survive without them," Richardson said. "If the satellites go, we'd be blacked out."

"Got it," Brendan said.

They made the long cruise as night fell. It was quiet.

"This is way larger than I expected, dude," Juan Carlos said.

"Normally this place would be thick with pleasure craft," Richardson said.

"You've spent time here with your girlfriend?" Brendan asked.

"Yeah," he said. "Great place."

"You serious about Lita?" Juan Carlos asked.

"I'm going to pop the question as soon as the war is over," Richardson said.

"Why not before?" Brendan asked.

"I've got enough to worry about," Richardson said. "I've got the feeling I won't live through this war."

"Gee, thanks, boss," Juan Carlos said.

"I didn't say anything about you guys," Richardson said.

"Yeah, but you're serving with us," Juan Carlos said.

"I won't be on the boat forever," Richardson said. "I'm just here filling in, remember?"

"Why are you so worried?" Brendan asked.

Richardson stood silently for a moment.

"Well?" Juan Carlos asked.

"There's half a million Islamists on the loose in Texas that we know about, with more flooding in all the time. Eventually we're going to end up fighting these people house to house. We don't have enough forces to defeat them."

"You're forgetting about the population," Brendan said.

"Oh, I know we got tons of people with guns, but few of them are well trained."

"They're more capable than you think," Brendan said. "Look what happened in Austin and Dripping Springs."

"That was when the war was just getting started," Richardson said. "Look at the reports on Carthage, Sonora, and Stonewall. Lots of dead civilians in all of those places, and the enemy forces that carried out those attacks are still operating."

"He's got a point, dude," Juan Carlos said.

"Those were all small towns that got caught with their pants down," Brendan said. "Wait and see what happens. These Islamists are going to run into a buzz saw when they try to take any of the major cities, or even any of the middle-sized cities."

"I pray that you're right," Richardson said. "Meanwhile we're on the front lines. You hear that?"

"Is that a prop plane?" Juan Carlos asked, scanning the skies.

"I'm calling it in," Richardson said. "Stay sharp."

"We can't fight aircraft very well," Brendan said as Richardson got on the radio.

"DPS Headquarters, come in please. Over." Richardson said.

"This is DPS Headquarters. Who is this speaking please? Over."

"Lieutenant Richardson in the southern patrol boat. We hear a prop plane approaching. Is it a friendly? Over."

"No, we have no prop planes in the air. Attempt to shoot it down. We'll notify the choppers. What is your position? Over."

"We're about five miles south of Port Mansfield. Over."

"Thank you. Over and out."

"It's getting closer," Juan Carlos said, turning the boat towards the noise, scanning the night sky.

"I don't see it yet," Brendan said. "Wait, there it is. It's an old seaplane. Look. Flying low over the water. Hard to see in the dark. Not running any lights."

"It's trying to stay under the radar," Richardson said. "Blast it."

Richardson and Brendan got on their .50 cals and started firing as Juan Carlos tried to follow it with the M19.

"It's moving too fast, dude," he yelled.

"Lead it and fire. As fast as you can. We've got plenty of grenades. The choppers will be here any second."

"Got it," Juan Carlos said, driving, his eyes still on the sight. He fired, the grenade flying past the front of the plane and exploding.

"More speed," Richardson yelled, as he and Brendan continued to fire. "We're not close enough."

"That's a plane, dude," Juan Carlos said, flooring the throttle. "We can't keep up with that thing." He fired off several more grenades.

"I hear the choppers," Brendan said.

"Look, the plane is turning this way!" Richardson shouted.

"Guns coming out of the side door," Brendan shouted. He looked over at Juan Carlos, who had his eyes in the sight, ignoring everything else.

"Come to papa," he said as the plane was in mid-turn, banking, exposing the top of its wing. He fired three grenades in rapid succession. The first two missed, but the third one hit the tail, blowing it off. The plane careened into the water, exploding on impact just as the choppers got overhead. They opened up with their mini-guns, shattering what was left of the plane as its hulk floated on the water.

"Nice shooting!" Brendan yelled.

"Took you too many rounds," Richardson said.

"I know, but I'll get better," Juan Carlos said. "Should we go over there?"

"Yeah, just in case there are survivors," Richardson said. "Maybe we can question them." Juan Carlos turned the boat back in the direction of the wreckage and sped up, arriving in a couple of minutes. Most of the plane had sunk by the time they got there.

"No survivors," Brendan said as he searched the area with spotlight next to his gun.

"Dammit," Richardson said. "We need to know who this was and what they were doing."

"Hope they didn't have a nuke on board," Brendan said.

"We'll get a dive team out here in the morning," Richardson said, picking up the mic. He called in the results to DPS Headquarters.

Martinis and Eggplant

Maria walked into Kip Hendrix's office. "Sir, Attorney General's office on the line." She had fear in her eyes.

"Good, I'll take it," Hendrix said. "Thanks, Maria."

He looked out the window into the late-afternoon sky, then hit the flashing button on his phone and put the receiver to his ear.

"Kip Hendrix."

"How goes it, Kip?"

"Fine, Franklin," he said. "How are you?"

"About the same. Wanted to share some intelligence with you."

"I'm all ears," Hendrix said.

"We intercepted a small plane outside of DC this morning. Tried to get it to land, but the pilot refused, and was heading towards the Mall area. We shot it down. It had a nuclear device in it."

"No shit," Hendrix said. "It didn't go off?"

"Pilot didn't get a chance to set it off."

"Good," Hendrix said.

"We got lucky. We aren't giving second chances anymore," Franklin said. "Usually we follow and don't shoot, especially over populated areas. Now we give one warning and fire."

"Were there casualties on the ground?"

"Yeah. Took out a couple of houses. Eight people killed, including a couple of kids."

"Dammit," Hendrix said, eyes misting. "There was a seaplane shot down by a DPS patrol boat by South Padre Island last night. We sent a dive team out there earlier. Haven't gotten word on what they found yet."

"South Padre Island, eh? That's not a good place for a nuclear device. Not enough people to kill around there."

"You wouldn't think so," Hendrix said. "One theory I heard was that the Coast Guard ships are too much of a threat to aircraft, so they took the route inside to get past them. Probably targeting Corpus Christi."

"Shit," Franklin said. "Glad you blasted them, in any event."

"Seriously," Hendrix said. "What else is going on? Heard you had some problems with martial law in upstate New York."

"Luddites," Franklin said. "The Governor of New York gave up. The President is furious."

"Why would he be so upset? Wasn't it a state matter?"

"He's changing the relationship of the Federal Government and the States," Franklin said. "You know that. We need more centralized control in order to get a handle on our gun problem. You were for it."

"Yeah, I remember," Hendrix said.

"You changed your mind?"

"I've become a realist," Hendrix said. "Getting guns away from the population is a pipe dream. It's not gonna happen. More Federal control isn't going to help. Just the opposite."

"Speaking of State's Rights, what can you tell me about Nelson's plans for New Mexico?"

"I haven't been involved in those discussions," Hendrix said.

"Watch it," Franklin said. "I just told you about the situation in New York."

"I already knew most of what you told me," Hendrix said. "I don't know why you're getting your panties in a bunch about this, anyway."

"We don't want Texas taking over territory," Franklin said. "Or pushing other States to follow Texas out of the union."

"I'm sure that isn't Nelson's intent."

"Then what is his intent?"

Hendrix sighed. "I guess I can tell you that much. New Mexico is getting a flood of foreign fighters, and the state government there is doing nothing about it. Nelson's just shoring up our border there, and if need be, chasing invaders into New Mexico."

"That's an attack on the sovereignty of the United States," Franklin said.

"So send Federal troops into New Mexico to clean up the mess," Hendrix said. "Texas has better things to do than clean up after you guys."

Franklin laughed. "The President would do that, if he wanted to."

Hendrix snickered. "Yeah, this is pretty funny when you think about it. Reminds me of how the European countries dealt with each other back in the middle ages."

"You sure you can't tell me anything else?"

"I can tell you this. Nelson has no interest in annexing New Mexico. I'm sure of that. No bullshit."

"Well I guess that's as much as I'll get for today. You may be asked for more in the future. We still have things to hold over your head."

"And I still don't care," Hendrix said. "Take your best shot, but this back channel has its own value. It'd be a shame to lose it by pushing too hard."

"Have it your way for now, Kip. Talk to you later."

"Take care," Hendrix said. Franklin hung up, and Hendrix slammed the receiver into its cradle. "What an asshole."

Maria rushed in. "Everything okay?"

Hendrix smiled at her, struggling to keep his eyes on her face. She was wearing a tight navy-blue dress, and she looked stunning.

"Don't worry," he said. "It's fine. I just hate dealing with that guy."

"He wanted to know things you couldn't tell him?" she asked.

"Yeah, the usual," Hendrix said. "I'm not going to budge. I can tell you all about it at dinner tonight."

"You sure it's a good idea for us to go out?" she asked.

"Having second thoughts?"

"I got a little out of hand last night." Maria said. "I was ashamed when I woke up this morning."

"You were fine," Hendrix said. "That was the best time I've had in months."

"I teased you," she said. "I shouldn't drink like that."

"Did I take advantage? Did I get mad?"

She looked at him, eyes softening. "No, sir. You were such a gentleman yesterday. In every way. You were perfect. It's me that I'm worried about."

"You were charming," Hendrix said. "I loved everything about yesterday. Especially when you were sleeping against me in the waiting room. It's so nice to feel protective of those we care about."

Maria saw the look of longing in his eyes, behind the smile. He loves me. Suddenly he no longer seemed like a lecherous old man to her, but she pushed that feeling back, her heart pounding.

"Are you okay?" Hendrix asked. "We don't have to go out tonight. It's up to you. Really. I know how worried you are about your sister."

"You'd be disappointed," she said

"I'm a grown-up," Hendrix said. "I can take it. We don't ever have to go out again if you don't want to."

She stood, looking at him, thinking, working out the possibilities, good and bad.

"If you're having to think that hard, maybe we better put it off," Hendrix said, trying to keep the disappointment from showing. She noticed it anyway.

"No, I think we should go," Maria said. "I'm sorry I'm such a stick in the mud. Yesterday was delightful, at least when we were done with my sister. I am worried about her, but I know she's safe for now. She can't hurt herself at the facility, and I'm not responsible for watching her. It's a big load off my mind."

"Great," Hendrix said. "I've only got another half hour before I can stop for the day. Do you want to go home and have me pick you up, or do you want to leave from here?"

"I think I'd better go home first and freshen up a bit," she said. "How nice should I dress?"

"What do you feel like eating?"

"Comfort food at somewhere quiet," she said. "It doesn't have to be too expensive."

"Italian?" Hendrix asked.

"That would be lovely," she said. "I can't drink red wine, though."

"Don't like it?"

"Allergic," she said. "I always get sick."

"No problem, the place I'm thinking about has cocktails too," he said.

She flashed an embarrassed smile. "I'll have to watch myself. Casual dress?"

"Smart casual," Hendrix said. "I wouldn't wear jeans and a t-shirt."

She giggled. "I wouldn't do that anyway."

"I'll pick you up at eight. Is that enough time?"

"It's just six now, so that'll be fine," she said.

"Go ahead and take off now if you'd like. I won't need you for what I have left to do."

"Okay," she said. "See you later. Thanks."

"Bye bye," he said. She turned and walked out the door, giving him a chance to take in her shape. His heart fluttered.

"Now back to business," he muttered to himself, picking up the phone receiver. He dialed Governor Nelson's private line and waited as it rang.

"Kip," Nelson said. "What's up?"

"Just got off the phone with Franklin," he said.

"Anything interesting?"

"He told me that they shot down a small plane outside of DC."

"Military?"

"No, it was a general aviation plane. Had a nuclear device on board."

"Dammit," Nelson said. "You heard about that seaplane that the DPS shot down last night, right?"

"Yeah," Nelson said. "It didn't have a nuke on it, I hope."

Nelson was quiet for a moment.

"Shit," Hendrix said.

"Not a word about this, okay Kip?"

"Understood. What was the target? There isn't much around South Padre Island."

"We're still trying to figure that out," Nelson said. "Of course some of our analysts are saying Corpus Christi, but we aren't so sure. That plane had enough range to get very close to Houston."

"They've already tried that once," Hendrix said.

"That's where our gasoline supply comes from, for the most part," Nelson said. "If we lose those refineries, we're in deep trouble."

"I figured," Hendrix said.

"He try to nudge you?"

"I was getting to that. He wanted to know all about our plans for New Mexico."

"Had a feeling."

"They think we're going to annex them or convince them to leave the union."

Nelson laughed. "We'll be lucky if they don't attack us for pursuing the bad guys past the border."

Hendrix chuckled. "I told them if the Feds would enforce the damn border down there we wouldn't be doing anything."

"You said that?" Nelson said, laughing. "I'll bet that was a shock."

"This mess has changed me from an open borders guy to a semi-open borders guy," Hendrix said.

"Semi-open borders, huh," Nelson said. "We'll have to chat about that, but not today. It's getting late, and my wife wants me home tonight. Thanks for the info, Kip. Take care."

"You too, Governor," Hendrix said. "Have a nice evening with your family."

Hendrix stood, wondering himself what he meant, how the chat would go. No matter. Maria. His excitement was building. Take it easy. Don't push too hard. He hurried out of the office suite, locking the main doors and heading to his car, getting home quickly. Shower, shave, dress. What makes me look the youngest? It took him forty-five minutes to decide and get dressed. A pause on the way out the door, quick look in the mirror. Not bad for an old guy. He arrived at Maria's apartment building just in time. She opened it after his knock, wearing a scoop-neck sweater and a mid-length silk skirt. Causal but lovely.

"You look great," he said.

"This top won't bother you? It's a little low cut, but it's the best thing I have to go with this skirt."

"Are you kidding?" Hendrix asked, smiling. "Sorry. I'll behave. Ready to go?"

"Sure. You look very nice yourself," Maria said, coming out the door and locking it. She took his arm and they headed for the car.

The restaurant was only half a mile away. He pulled into the parking lot.

"Oh, I've been here before," she said. "It's a great place."

"Yeah, it's quiet and the food's good. The bartender is great."

"They know you here like they did at the place yesterday?" she asked.

"No," he said. "I don't get here that often. There's an Italian place that I like a lot closer to my house."

"We could've gone there."

"I didn't want a long drive back and forth to your place, in case I have a cocktail or two."

"Oh," she said. He got out of the car and hurried around, opening her door for her. She took his hand, looking embarrassed as they touched, but only for a moment.

"It's pretty dead tonight," Hendrix said.

"It is," she said as they waited at the hostess station. "It's a zoo on the weekends. Big date place."

"I could imagine," Hendrix said. The hostess showed up.

"Two?" she asked.

"Yes, at a quiet booth if you've got it," Hendrix said.

"Of course," she said, pulling two menus out of the holder. "Follow me."

They went to the back, to a dimly lit booth with a candle burning on the table. It was an oval booth, big enough for four people.

"This is perfect," Hendrix said, sliding in on one side. Maria slid into the other side.

"There's hardly anybody back here," Maria said. "Even less than a usual weeknight."

"People may be afraid to go out," Hendrix said. "You know how it's been."

"There haven't been attacks around here," she said. "Hope that doesn't change."

"I don't expect any here," he said. "Austin might be the safest place to be right now."

"I hope so," she said. "We're almost on the outskirts."

"True," he said, "but I think we'll be fine."

The waitress walked over. She was wearing a tight, low-cut red dress, sporting short bleach-blonde hair and hoop earrings.

"Hi, I'm Cat," she said. "Can I get y'all something from the bar?"

"There's a drink menu," Hendrix said, pulling it out of its stand and sliding it to Maria. She opened it and looked.

"What are you having?" Maria asked.

"My usual," Hendrix said. "A gin martini, up with olives."

"You think I'd like one of those?" she asked.

"Do you like gin?" Cat asked.

"I don't know," Maria said.

"How about this," Hendrix said, looking at Cat. "Bring me one. I'll let her have a sip. If she doesn't like it, she can order something else."

"We can do that," Cat said.

"Okay, let's do it," Maria said.

"Coming right up," Cat said, turning to leave.

"That's quite a dress," Maria whispered, watching her walk away. "Pretty low cut if she has to bend over the table. Not that you'd mind, of course."

Hendrix smiled at her as she giggled. "I'm not gonna lie."

"That's why I wasn't sure about wearing this," she said.

"You look lovely," Hendrix said.

"Thank you," she said. "Maybe I should look in the drink menu for what I might want if the martini isn't it."

"There are a lot of flavored martini drinks," Hendrix said. "Chocolate, apple, cranberry, and so on.

"Oh, yeah, I see them here. Are they a lot like your martini?"

"They're made with vodka instead of gin," Hendrix said, "and they're flavored pretty heavily. You don't taste the alcohol."

"That sounds dangerous," she said, eyes dancing.

"You know what they call those drinks, right?"

"No," she said, studying him. "It's going to be naughty, I'll bet."

"Leg openers," Hendrix said, a sly smile on his face.

"That's naughty all right," she said, face flushing. "Why, because women drink them too fast?"

"Yeah," Hendrix said. "They aren't any stronger than a gin martini, but they go down a lot quicker and easier, especially for somebody who isn't used to drinking."

"Oh, you mean people like me," she said.

"No, I didn't say that," he said. "I think the target audience for those drinks is women who've just turned twenty-one."

Cat returned and slid the gin martini in front of Maria. "There you go. Have a sip."

"You sure?" Maria asked.

"Please," Hendrix said.

She took a sip and left it in her mouth for a moment, eyes lighting up. "Wow, this is good. Very refreshing. Not too sweet."

"Yes, they're great. I love the olives too. Take a bite of one and sip a little."

She pulled the stick out and bit half of the olive, then took a sip. "You're right, it's heavenly. I'll have one of these."

"I'll tell you what," Cat said. "If you order a pitcher, I'll give you that first one on the house."

Hendrix thought about it for a moment. "What do you think, Maria?"

"Is it going to get us too drunk?" she asked, looking concerned.

"It might if we drink it all, but we don't have to," Hendrix said.

"Price-wise, it's worth it even if you leave a drink or two," Cat said.

"Okay, let's do it," Hendrix said.

"Coming right up," Cat said. She turned and left. Maria started to slide the martini over to Hendrix.

"No, no, go ahead," he said. "She'll be back with the pitcher in a moment."

"Okay," she said. She had another sip, bigger this time. "Wow, I can feel it behind my eyes."

Hendrix studied her as she enjoyed the feeling. Her eyes met his and he felt he was going to melt. He teared up a little.

"What's wrong?" she asked.

"I'm just happy to be with you," Hendrix said. "Sorry, us guys get more emotional as we get older."

"You're full of surprises," she said, taking another sip. "This is so good. You want a sip at least?"

"Here comes Cat now," Hendrix said. She carried a tray with the pitcher and a glass stir stick, a bowl of olives, a few olive sticks, and a glass sitting in a bucket.

"Here we go," Cat said, putting it all on the table between them. "Enjoy. Ready to order yet?"

"Shoot, we haven't even opened the menus yet," Maria said, smiling.

"Give us a little while, okay?" Hendrix asked.

"Y'all take as much time as you need," Cat said. "I'll be back in a little while."

"Thanks," Hendrix said. He watched her walk away, ample figure straining against the tight dress.

Maria giggled as she watched him looking. "Hey, don't make me jealous."

"No fair," he said. "I'm not allowed to look at you that way, remember?" Hendrix chuckled as he poured his martini from the pitcher and stuck a few olives on a stick.

Maria smiled and took another big sip of her drink. "Oh, all right, you can look at me that way here. Just not at work, okay? And don't leer so much that people see it."

"I'd never think of it," he said. He took his first sip. "Perfect."

"What's in the bucket?" she asked.

"Ice, so we can chill the glasses."

"Oh," she said, taking the last sip. She ate the rest of her olive.

"Ready for some more?" Hendrix asked.

"I shouldn't, but yes." She slid her glass towards him. "I'm too far away. Mind if I move to the middle of the booth?"

"I'd love it," Hendrix said as he put her glass into the ice bucket.

She tried to scoot over, leaning forward too far, feeling her scoop neck open. She raised a hand to it and then had trouble getting around. She glanced at him. "Oh, what the hell." She took her hand away and finished moving, glancing up to see if he looked. His eyes were focused on pouring her martini.

"Here you go," he said, handing it to her and dropping in a stick with olives.

"You just missed it," she said as she took a sip.

"That would have been taking advantage," he said.

She giggled and took another sip. "You keep passing my tests."

"Is that what they are?" he asked, taking a sip, savoring the flavor. He felt it rushing to his brain. "So what do I get for passing?"

She sighed, then reached over across the table, pretending to grab for his menu, feeling her sweater gape open, holding her position. "There" she whispered.

Hendrix looked, the tops of her breasts hanging before him in white lacy bra cups. He moaned, and she sat back up, shooting him a mischievous glance.

"I know, that was way too naughty," she said, having another sip. "Wow, I can really feel this."

"Slow down a little if you need to," Hendrix said.

"But it tastes so good," she said. "You don't look like it's hitting you at all."

"You're ahead of me," he said, "and women get hit harder, too."

"Well, drink up," she said. "I don't want to be the only one acting silly."

Hendrix chuckled. "Don't worry, I'm sure you won't be. I can already feel it hitting me." He looked at her again, taking in her form sitting next to him, from her butt up to her beautiful face.

"Caught you," she said.

"You said I could," he said.

"I know," she said, eyes dancing again.

"Maria! I think you're enjoying this."

"Maybe a little," she said softly.

"Good," Hendrix said. "Maybe we'd better look at the menus. We need a little food to counteract these drinks."

"Okay," she said. "Should I reach for yours again?"

"You really know how to torture me, don't you?" he said as she stretched towards his menu again.

"Is it really torture?"

"Oh, God," he whispered as he looked.

"That's enough," she said, sitting up with the menu in her hands. She opened it and slid closer, so their hips were touching. "Let's share."

"Yes, let's," he said, putting his hand on her thigh, close to the knee. She jumped, and he moved his hand away quickly. "Sorry."

"Don't be silly," she said, grabbing his hand and putting it back. "Now, focus on the menu."

"I already know what I want," he said.

"On the menu, I hope."

He looked at her and smiled. "Yes, on the menu."

"Oh," she said. "What?"

"Eggplant Parmesan," he said. "It's good here."

"That does sound good," she said. "With garlic bread."

"Of course," Hendrix said. "See, I can focus, even in the most difficult of circumstances."

She giggled. "You can be so much fun, Kip." She put her hand to her mouth. "Have I ever called you that before?"

"No," Hendrix said, "but I liked it."

"I'll never call you that at work," she said.

Cat came over. "Looks like you two lovebirds are getting cozy. Liking those martinis?"

"Very good," Hendrix said. "I think we're ready to order."

"What will it be?"

"Eggplant Parmesan and garlic bread," Maria said.

"For both of you, right?"

"Yes, please," Hendrix said.

"Okay, we'll get that started for y'all." She took the menus and turned to walk away.

"You didn't look at her this time," Maria said as their eyes locked.

"I only have eyes for you," Hendrix said. "Oh, that was terrible."

She chuckled as Hendrix put his empty glass in the ice bucket.

"Having more, are you," she said.

"I haven't caught up with you yet," he said. He took the chilled glass out of the ice and poured himself another. "I love these. One of the best inventions of mankind."

"They are good," she said. "Maybe I'll hate myself in the morning, though."

"Why?" Hendrix asked.

"Hangover," she said. "Wait, what did you think I was talking about?"

"Hangover, of course," he said, grinning.

"Liar," she said. "Hey, what were you going to tell me?"

"Work talk?" he asked, faking disappointment.

"Only for a few minutes," she said, eyes dilated. "What?"

"This is another one you can't tell anybody. Nelson told me specifically not to spread it around."

"You can trust me," she said, putting her hand on his thigh.

"All right," he whispered. "Small planes have become a worry."

"How?" she asked, looking nervous.

"One was shot down on the way into DC yesterday," he said. "There was a nuclear device on board."

"Oh, my God," she said, looking horrified. "It didn't go off, did it?"

"No, they won't go off from concussion," Hendrix said. "They had to shoot it down over a residential neighborhood. Some people got killed." He choked up, his eyes tearing. "Eight people died, including a couple of kids."

"Oh, honey," she said, touching his cheek. "This really bothers you."

"Sorry," he said, wiping his eyes. "It's the kids."

"Why was I scared of you?" she muttered to herself.

"Because I wasn't appropriate at work," Hendrix said. He pulled himself together. "That wasn't the whole story."

"You don't have to go on," she said, hand still on his cheek, eyes locked.

"It's okay, the rest is easier," he said. "I got that info from the contact at the Attorney General's office."

"Oh," she said. "Really?"

"Yeah, this back-channel thing they have me doing is working pretty well. Anyway, I called Governor Nelson right after the call and told him about the conversation. He told me that a seaplane was shot down by a DPS patrol boat last night, in the bay behind South Padre Island. It had a device in it too."

"Oh, geez," she said. "Are we gonna get killed?"

"Not if I can help it," Hendrix said.

She leaned against him, hand back on his thigh. "I do feel safe with you," she said, "but this is getting really crazy." They sat that way for several minutes, enjoying the quiet closeness.

"Maybe y'all should get a room," Cat said, standing there with their food.

"Sorry," Hendrix said, sitting up.

"Don't say that," Cat said. "Wish I had what you two have. I can feel it from across the room."

Maria looked at Hendrix with a sheepish smile as Cat set the entrees and the garlic bread basket down in front of them. "Still working on the martinis?"

"Well?" Hendrix asked.

"I think I've had more than enough," Maria said, smiling. "Those really are rocket fuel."

"I'll just finish the one I've got," Hendrix said. "You can take the rest."

"Okay," Cat said, putting it on her tray. She walked away.

"She thinks we're lovers," Maria whispered as she put her napkin on her lap.

"Sorry," Hendrix said. "I didn't mean to embarrass you. I should have corrected her."

"Why?" Maria asked. "She doesn't know us. This is interesting to me."

"Interesting? Why?"

"Nobody is batting an eye at our difference in age," she said.

"Oh," Hendrix said. He took a bite of dinner. "Great as usual."

She took a bite and her eyes lit up. "This is good." She reached for the garlic bread, offering it to him. He took a piece, then she did the same and put it back.

They ate silently for a few minutes, both deep in thought.

"Hear anything about your sister?" Hendrix asked.

"I talked to the facility before you got to my place," Maria said. "She's stable. That's all they would tell me."

"Where's her facility?"

"Pretty close to work, actually. Near the city center," she said, glancing at him, then looking away quickly. "This food pretty much killed my buzz."

"You want some of mine?" he asked.

"No, I'm glad my head is getting clear again," she said.

"You think we got too carried away," Hendrix said.

She looked into his eyes. "I didn't say that. I want to see if it's still here after I'm a little sobered up."

"What?"

"The feeling that started when you cried about those kids," she said softly.

"Oh," Hendrix said, taking a sip of water. "Sorry to get emotional like that."

"You don't get it, do you?" she asked.

Suddenly there was a boom outside, in the distance. Hendrix's eyes got wide and he snapped himself out of the daze Maria had him in. "That sounded like artillery fire!"

"Oh no," Maria said, trembling.

There were two more booms, and a couple of explosions. The building rumbled.

"Kip!" she cried, looking at him.

"C'mon, let's get out of here," he said, taking a hundred-dollar bill out of his wallet and throwing it on the table. "Ought to be enough."

Maria grabbed her purse and took Hendrix's arm as they raced for the door. Outside was pandemonium, people running back and forth. There were more booms, closer now, explosions less than a block away, approaching from the south.

"We need to leave now," Hendrix said, taking her hand and running to his Mercedes. He used remote start and helped her into the passenger seat, then ran to the driver's seat, taking off with tires squealing, heading for South Congress Avenue, punching it as the cannon fire intensified, weaving in and out of traffic in a panic.

"You okay to drive?" she asked.

"Yeah," he said. "No problem."

Maria looked out the rear window. "Is that a tank?" There was another boom, blowing up a building just behind them to the right.

Hendrix checked the rear-view mirror. "My God, that's an M-1. Son of a bitch."

"Can they catch us?"

"No way," Hendrix said.

"I can't go back to my apartment, can I?"

"Not tonight," Hendrix said. "We're going to my place. I've got a compound northwest of the State Capitol. It's got a bunker, high walls, and a security system."

"How'd you get that?"

"Part of the position," Hendrix said. "It belongs to Texas."

"It won't protect us against that, will it?"

"The bunker will," he said. "I'll take you somewhere else if you don't want to go with me."

"You're kidding, right?" she said, looking at him. He was focused on the road as she watched him drive. His steely reserve calmed her, then warmed her. "My God," she whispered.

"What?" Hendrix asked. "Something else happen?"

"No," she said. "It's just me."

{ 18 }

The Homestead

Kim's eyes darted around nervously as Eric drove the rig.

"You sure this is gonna be safe?" she asked as they rolled down the dark country road. They'd been on back roads, some of them dirt, for hours.

"It's too late to go anywhere else," Eric said. "It'll be dark in a hurry, and we know Sonora isn't safe."

"Doesn't it bother you to be here, after what happened to your parents?"

"The house might, but we don't have to go inside," Eric said. "There's several acres to park on, and there's hookups out by the barn, according to Jason."

"You going to call him?"

"No," Eric said. "His phone might have been compromised again, and we don't want to reveal our location. I'll call him when we leave tomorrow."

"Skinny road," Kim said as they got to the switchbacks. "Hope nobody's coming in the other direction."

Eric's phone rang. He handed it to Kim. "Put it on speaker. I need both hands on the wheel right now."

Kim nodded and answered it, pushing the speaker button. "Hey Dirk, got you on speaker."

"Where the hell are we going? This is a scary road."

"My parent's house," Eric said. "We can overnight here. Maybe pick up some supplies too."

"The enemy knows about this place," Dirk said.

"That's true, but I doubt they've got somebody here watching it just in case somebody returns. They've got bigger fish to fry. Watch the phone usage, just in case."

"Roger that," Dirk said. "How much further?"

"Ten minutes," Eric said. "The road gets better shortly. Once we get down into the valley."

"Good, this is hairy. Glad it's not quite dark yet."

"Talk to you guys later," Eric said.

"Later," Dirk said. Kim ended the call.

"It's pretty back here at least," she said.

"It is," Eric said. "I was already half-way out when my folks got this place, so I didn't live here much." His face was grim.

"Thinking about your falling-out with your dad?"

"Yeah," Eric said. "Seems so stupid now."

The road got back down to the valley floor and widened.

"What a peaceful little valley," Kim said, looking around in the dusk.

"We'll be able to see the house in a few minutes," Eric said, turning on the headlights. "Almost dark."

They rode silently along the bumpy road until they saw the house.

"There it is," Eric said.

"Rustic."

"There's still police tape around the front door," Eric said, eyes getting glassy.

"You sure you'll be able to handle this?"

"I'm sure, honey," he said, looking at her for a moment. "I'm going to park by the barn." He turned into the driveway and drove to the large flat section in front of the barn, circling so he was pointed back at the driveway, making enough room for Dirk's rig and the Suburban to pull in.

Paco trotted over and whined, jumping up at Eric's seat.

"Okay, pal, we'll take you out right away. I know it's been a while."

"I'll get his leash and a flashlight," Kim said, getting out of her seat.

"Hope the power's still on," Eric said as he followed her. They hooked up Paco and went out the side door.

"Nice spread," Dirk said as he got out of his truck.

"Yeah," Eric said. My folks had a good setup here. I'll see if I can get the power turned on."

Eric and Kim approached the house.

"You got keys?" Kim asked.

"I know where my dad always hides a set," Eric said. "Hopefully Jason didn't take them."

He walked to the side door. It had yellow police tape tacked in front of it in a crisscross fashion.

"The eave over the door," Eric said. "Hold the leash for a minute."

Kim took it, watching as Eric reached up on top of the wood frame of the door. He came down with keys in his hand.

"Good," Kim said.

Eric pulled the tape away from the door and unlocked it. "Here goes nothing." He opened the door, reaching around to switch on the kitchen lights. Nothing.

"Maybe it's just the main breaker," Kim said.

"I hope so," Eric said. "It's around the back. Follow me."

They walked to the back of the house, Eric shining the flashlight at the wall, stopping at the rectangular box with the glass dome above.

"That it?" Kim asked.

"Yeah." Eric opened the cover and shined the light in. "Main breaker is off." He switched it on, and the kitchen light flooded out onto the driveway.

"Yes!" Kim said.

"There's flood lights by the barn that will light up this whole area," Eric said. "C'mon."

They walked to the barn and found the switch. Eric flipped it on and the whole area lit up.

"Perfect," Kim said.

Eric reached into the barn and turned the lights on inside. "Let's go check out the house, okay?"

"Should we take Paco back to the coach?"

"No, we need his eyes and ears." Eric said, leading her to the side door. They walked into the lighted kitchen.

"Not so rustic in the kitchen," Kim said. "This is nice. They remodeled it, obviously."

"Somebody cleaned it," Eric said. "I'll bet it was some of his friends on Fredericksburg PD."

He walked into the living room. It was in good shape too, the furniture and lamps covered with plastic sheeting. Eric uncovered a big lamp inside the door and turned it on. Paco sniffed around.

"They had a dog?" Kim asked.

"Yeah, Dingo," Eric said. "Australian Shepherd. Jason has him now."

"Paco can smell him," Kim said, watching him.

"That hallway goes to the bedrooms," Eric said.

"Where did they find your parents?"

"In the master, lying in bed," Eric said. "C'mon."

"Maybe you shouldn't go in there."

"It'll be okay," Eric said, walking into the hallway. He switched on the hall light. The first bedroom was set up as an office. Further down was a bathroom, and another bedroom set up as a guest room. The final door, at the end of the hall, was the master. Eric paused for a moment before switching on the light.

"You sure?" Kim asked.

"I'm okay, sweetie," he said, switching on the light just inside the door.

"Good, the bed's gone," Kim said.

"And the carpet," Eric said, looking down at the old hardwood, tac strips still there. "They cleaned things out pretty well. Makes it a lot easier."

"Could you ever live here?" Kim asked.

"Yeah, I think I could," Eric said. "Might happen if we stay in Texas. Good place to raise kids. What do you think?"

"It might be difficult for you after a while."

"I don't believe in ghosts," he said.

"I wasn't talking about ghosts," Kim said, "but never mind. What next?"

"Let's go check out the RV hookup situation," Eric said. "I'll let Dirk use it. He might need it more than we do. Then maybe we can gather in here and watch the TV. I'd like to see some news."

"Okay," she said. "Let's go."

They left the lights on in the house and walked to the rigs.

"There's the hookup," Eric said, pointing to a covered electrical box on the side of the barn. He flipped up the cover. "Wow, fifty amps. Nice."

"I'll put Paco inside and feed him, honey," Kim said.

"Okay," he said, walking over to Dirk and the others.

"House check out okay?" Francis asked.

"Yeah," Eric said. "I'll fire up the TV so we can catch up on some news. There's an RV electrical hookup right there. You guys need to plug in your trailer for a while?"

"Probably be a good idea," Dirk said. "Doesn't charge very well while I'm driving."

"What are you running?" Eric asked.

"Thirty amp," he said. "I got an adapter for fifty amp output, though."

"Good, bring it over here," Eric said, walking towards the box. "Your cable reach this far?"

"Yeah, should," Dirk said. "Thanks. You don't need it?"

"Nah, my batteries are full," he said. "If we were staying more than one night, I'd need to plug in."

"Okay," Dirk said. "Thanks. When are you going to watch TV?"

"Give me about ten minutes. We can use the kitchen in the house to cook."

Eric went into the coach. Kim was sitting on the couch, looking at the browser on her phone, face grim.

"What are you seeing?" he asked as he sat next to her.

"Rumors on the message boards," she said. "Scary rumors."

"What?"

"Tanks rolling into Austin from the south."

"Shit," Eric said. "I figured they'd stay in the small towns for a while. Anything official? Maybe it's just the usual web BS."

"Nothing official," Kim said. "It'll be interesting to see if anything shows up on the news tonight. Where we sleeping?"

"I'm okay with sleeping in here," Eric said. "but if you want to take that guest room in the house, fine with me."

"Let's see how the evening goes," Kim said. "There's two couches in that living room, too."

"Ready to go over?" Eric asked.

"What do you want to eat?"

"We can zap some frozen stuff in the kitchen," Eric said. "We still have a pretty good assortment."

"Okay," she said. "Let's do that. How about Paco?"

"We take him," Eric said.

"Good," Kim got off the couch and went to the fridge, looking in the freezer. "There's a couple of Italian meals."

"Fine. I like everything we have, so just grab me whatever."

She nodded as Eric put the leash back on Paco. "Want me to bring any beer?"

"Nah, I want to stay straight," Eric said. "You go ahead, though."

Kim laughed. "After that Southern Comfort last night, the thought of drinking makes me queasy."

He chuckled and opened the coach door. They walked out into the bright light of the floods and headed for the kitchen door.

"Shall I zap these now?" Kim asked.

"Might as well, since the fridge has been off," Eric said. "Take a while to cool it down."

"That's what I was thinking," Kim said.

"I'll go uncover the rest of the furniture in the front room and turn on the TV."

Francis and Sherry walked in, carrying a big frozen lasagna. "The oven working?" Sherry asked.

"Yeah, should be," Eric said. "It's electric."

"Works for me," she said. "You guys are welcome to have some of this."

"We're zapping some meals," Kim said, "but thanks."

Sherry turned on the oven as Don and Chance walked in.

"You guys drinking tonight?" Don asked.

"Not me," Eric said. "Too nervous."

"Good, I thought it was just me," Chance said.

"Where's Dirk?" Kim asked.

"Looking for his power adapter," Don said. "His storage compartment is pretty full."

Alyssa and Chloe walked inside, nodding to everybody.

"Nice house," Alyssa said. "Anywhere we can sleep in here? The back of the SUV is getting a little old."

"There's a guest room, down the hall off the living room. It's got two twin beds and a sofa sleeper. Help yourselves."

"There's also two couches and a couple recliners in the living room, too," Kim said.

"Now girls, you let Eric and Kim have the guest room if they want it," Don said.

"It's fine," Eric said. "We're comfortable in our rig."

Kim nodded in agreement.

"I'll turn on the TV," Eric said, walking into the living room. He finished pulling the plastic off the furniture and set it in the corner, then found the TV remote. He looked at it closely, seeing the worn buttons and lettering. "Daddy," he muttered to himself, feeling the tears again.

"You all right?" Kim asked, coming up behind him.

"Yeah," he said, pushing the power button. The TV came on after a few seconds. He switched it to the local news channel. The video was showing aftermath of the Stonewall attack.

"The Stonewall death toll sits at sixty-three," the news woman said. "Nearly a hundred people are in hospitals all over the surrounding area, many of them in critical condition."

"Good lord," Sherry said, watching from the doorway to the kitchen. "They get all the bad guys?"

"Good question," Eric said. "Haven't said yet, but the tanks are all blown up. Not much left of the town."

Alyssa walked out from the guest room, staring at the devastation on TV. "Is that what happened in that town we had to go around?" She looked terrified.

"Yeah, sweetie," Sherry said. "Don't worry, they're a long way from here."

Don walked in. "You okay, honey?"

"Yeah, dad. I'm going to go get my speaker, okay?" she asked. "Chloe and I want to listen to some music in the guest room."

"Not too loud, okay?"

"We'll be quiet, dad," she said. "Thanks. Hey, Chloe!"

"Coming," Chloe said as she emerged from the hall. They walked into the kitchen and out the side door.

"Where are they going?" Dirk asked as he walked into the living room.

"Alyssa wants her speaker," Don said. "They're going to play music in the guest room."

"Oh," he said. "Found that damn adapter. It was really buried. Don't know what I was thinking. Shit, that Stonewall?"

"Yeah," Eric said. "It's a mess. I'll turn the sound up." He pointed the remote at the screen.

"Highway 290 remains closed between Johnson City and Fredericksburg. Portions west of Fredericksburg are also considered to be unsafe at this hour, as are parts of I-10."

"Dammit," Eric said. "Those are the two routes we can take."

"You know, this is pretty remote," Chance said. "Maybe we ought to fortify this place a little bit and hang out for a while."

"I want to join my brother," Eric said.

"He might have the right idea, honey," Kim said softly. "Wouldn't hurt for a few days."

Eric thought about it for a moment.

"Crap, what's going on now?" Don asked, nodding at the TV. The breaking news banner was stretched across the entire screen.

"This video is coming to you live from our helicopter over southern Austin. Tanks have come into town and are blowing up buildings and mowing down civilians."

"Daddy," Alyssa said, standing in the doorway with her speaker in her hand. "Are they gonna get us?"

"No, sweetie," Don said as she came over to him, Chloe right behind her.

"Son of a bitch," Eric said, watching the screen with wide eyes as the tanks moved along, cannons firing, buildings exploding.

"Eric," Kim said, trembling. He rushed to her, taking her into his arms. "What are we gonna do?"

"I count thirteen tanks," Dirk said. "Look at how fast they're moving. They're heading towards the State Capitol area."

"They've got a long way to go before they get that far," Chance said. "And the city gets denser. Slower going."

"They could lob shells that far now," Dirk said. "If they wanted to."

"I need to talk to Jason," Eric said. "Wonder if the land line still works here." He got up and went to the kitchen. The old wall phone was still next to the fridge. He picked up the receiver and put it to his ear. "Got a dial tone."

"You think it's safer to call your brother with that?" Kim asked.

"Yeah, they have a problem with land line calls – even land line to cell phone. I'm calling him now." He pulled out his iPhone and looked up Jason's number, then punched it into the keypad on the wall phone. It rang three times, and clicked.

"Jason," Eric said. "Don't say where I am."

"Thank God. We were afraid you got snagged in that mess at Stonewall."

"We went way out of the way to get around it. We're staying put for a while. Can't use 290 or I-10. You see what's going on in Austin?"

"No, I was just about to go to sleep."

"Turn on your TV. Southern Austin is under attack. Tanks. We counted thirteen on the video feed."

"Oh, God," Jason said, silent for a moment. "I see it."

"Anything bad happen there since last time we talked?"

"No, things are okay here, so far," Jason said. "Be careful staying where you are. They know about it."

"I know, that's why I used the land line. This place is defensible. I think we might stick around for a while."

"Well, if things get bad here, maybe we'll end up there. We're out in the open, too close to the interstate. If we didn't have our toys guarding us, we'd probably already be gone."

"I hear ya," Eric said. "I'm gonna get off the line. Take care of yourself."

"You too, bro," he said.

Eric hung up the phone and came back out. "What's happening?"

"A police armored vehicle came too close just now," Chance said. "It's splattered all over the place."

"Oh no," Eric said.

"Why aren't they doing something about this?" Alyssa asked, eyes wide.

"They will," Dirk said. "They'll bring in planes. It's the only way."

"That will kill a lot of people," Sherry said, eyes filling with tears.

"Yeah, it will," Francis said, pulling her closer. "No choice at this point."

"This is how the Europeans felt during World War II," Kim said. "Never thought we'd see that here."

"They have a limited supply of tanks," Eric said.

"Ground troops," Dirk said, rushing over to the TV screen and pointing. See. They're mopping up, killing people hidden in the rubble."

"My God, look how many there are," Kim said.

Everybody was silent for a while, just watching the carnage as the tanks and enemy fighters worked their way north. Then there was a bright flash on the video, and one of the tanks blew up.

"Jets," Dirk said. "About frigging time."

More bright flashes followed, and then some Apache helicopters came into view, circling above the scattering enemy fighters, miniguns blazing. One of them blew up.

"Damn, they've got stingers," Chance said.

Kim looked at Eric, teary eyed and trembling. He held her close.

"Can we stay here?" she asked.

"Yes," Eric said. "I got Jason. They might even end up here. They're too exposed in Fort Stockton."

"Good, I was hoping you'd say that," Don said. "I was looking at that barn. We could fit all our vehicles in there."

"We could," Eric said.

"There a back way in here, Eric?" Dirk asked.

"Not without off-roaders. Like Jeeps or Broncos, and even those would be tough. There's a pretty big creek blocking the way, and some gnarly hills."

"Good, because that thin section of road is very defendable," Dirk said. "It's between a big cliff and a mountainside."

"Any neighbors around?" Chance asked.

"There's a ranch on the other side of the little valley," Eric said. "Cattle and horses."

"You know the owners?" Dirk asked.

"I know who was here. Not sure if they still are. The Merchant family. Old man and his wife, three daughters. Middle one is about my age, one's several years older, and one a couple years younger. There was a brother, too, but he passed away before they moved here. Have no idea how many of the kids still live at home."

"They good folks?" Francis asked.

"Yeah, but they keep to themselves." Eric chuckled. "There were rumors that they were making white lighting. Don't know if it's true or not."

"The video's gone," Kim said, pointing to the TV.

"We're sorry, but we had to shut down the video feed, by order of the Texas National Guard," the commentator said. "We are still watching the situation with units on the ground."

"They don't want to show the carnage," Dirk said. "That won't matter too much longer."

Secure Locations

Maria's heart was finally slowing down, but she still scanned the mayhem through the rear window of the SUV, expecting to see an enemy vehicle in hot pursuit.

"We're far enough away now," Hendrix said, racing north up South Congress Avenue. "Damn, look at the fire back there."

"My apartment might be toast," Maria said. "Imagine if I wouldn't have come out with you tonight."

"I was just thinking that," Hendrix said. "I don't think I could've taken losing you."

He glanced at her, seeing her glassy eyes staring at him.

"Watch the road," she said quickly.

"Yeah," he said, still driving fast, weaving around slower vehicles. Now the air was filled with sirens, police and fire department vehicles racing down the southbound side of the street.

"Those tanks are gonna blow them up," Maria said.

"The Air National Guard will have to handle this," Hendrix said, glancing at her again as she wiped tears out of her eyes. "You okay?"

"I'm fine," she said, voice trembling.

A strange sounding alarm went off on his phone.

"What's that?" Maria asked.

"Emergency signal," Hendrix said. He fished his phone out of his pocket and looked at it. "Gotta pull over for a moment." He swerved over to the side and typed a text message, then hit send.

"What now?"

"I told them I was almost to the bunker, and that it'll be open. Might end up with company tonight."

"Who?" she aside.

"Other government people who are too far away from the other facilities," he said.

"Oh," she said. "I didn't know all this existed."

Hendrix watched his phone until it dinged with an acceptance message, then drove back onto the road.

"How much further?" Maria asked.

"We go up to 15th Street and make a left. Then it's just a few miles," he said. "We're away from the trouble now, at least. I can barely hear the cannon fire."

"It's still going, though," she said. "All those poor people. We gonna be able to stop this?"

"Yeah," Hendrix said. "I expect to hear some fireworks pretty soon, now that the emergency message went out."

"Oh, geez," Maria said.

"Where's your mom?"

"She lives north of Lake Travis," Maria said. "Hope Celia is safe."

"She should be okay," Hendrix said. "If she's near the capitol, she's probably in that big medical section next to I-35."

"Yeah, I think that's where she is," Maria said.

"There's 15th Street," Hendrix said, turning left. The road was empty. He sped up, glancing over at Maria again. She was staring but looked away quickly.

"I don't feel those drinks at all now," she said.

"Me neither," Hendrix said. "Funny how adrenaline will shove that out of your system so fast. You feeling okay?"

"Tired and scared," Maria said. "Good thing this didn't start half an hour earlier. We were pretty trashed."

Hendrix chuckled. "Yeah, we were, but I was having such a nice time."

"Me too," she said. "A little embarrassing when I think about it now."

"Why, because we got flirty?"

She was quiet for a moment. Hendrix glanced at her as she stared at him. She didn't look away this time.

"I'm sorry if I made you uncomfortable," he said. Then he heard her sniffling. "Oh no, I really blew it, didn't I? I'm so sorry."

"We have to talk later," she said quietly. "After we get there."

"I was trying so hard not to blow it," he said softly.

"Just drive," she said. "It'll be fine."

He gripped the wheel, full of regret, and kept his eyes on the road.

There was a large explosion to the south, the sky lighting up bright. Then another, and another.

"My God," Maria said.

"Scratch some tanks," Hendrix said. "I hope the civilians got far enough away from that."

"Me too," she said.

"There's my place," Hendrix said, turning into the long driveway and hitting the remote on his visor. A heavy-looking gate rolled to the side and they drove in. It closed quickly behind them.

"That's beautiful," Maria said, looking at the colonial revival house. Hendrix drove in the back, hitting another remote. The garage door opened and he pulled inside, hitting the button again to close it.

He took a deep breath and looked at her. "Welcome to my place. Sorry it isn't under better circumstances."

"I'm glad to be here," she said. Hendrix got out and opened the door for her.

"We have to go into the bunker first," Hendrix said. "I have to start up the systems and check in."

"Okay." She grabbed his hand and walked with him to the door, which he unlocked. They walked into a small hallway. There was an elevator door to the right. Hendrix put a key into the slot on the console next to the elevator and turned it, the doors opening within a few seconds. They got in and Hendrix pushed the button to take them down to the bunker.

"This doesn't go upstairs, does it?" Maria asked.

"No, this is just for the bunker. It's a hardened elevator. The bunker is sealed. It can take a nuclear blast pretty close by and survive."

"Wow," she said, getting closer to him. The doors opened into a hallway. Hendrix walked to the door just across from the elevator and input a code on the keypad. There was the sound of a seal breaking, and the door opened. It was heavy, like a bank vault.

"Geez," Maria said, looking at it.

"I know, always thought this was a huge waste of money," Hendrix said. "It's old, built in the 1950s." He showed her in, then went to a console to the right, just inside the door. He turned on the monitor and slid out a keyboard tray, inputting a password and waiting. The screen came up and he clicked several check boxes on the touch-screen monitor and touched a button that said "CONFIRM" on it.

"What does that do?" she asked.

"It tells the state's emergency system that we're here and open for business," he said. He turned on a bank of monitors next to the PC station. They showed video feeds of the front gate, the driveway inside, and the garage.

"So how long until people start showing up?" Maria asked, following him to a door on the opposite wall.

"Could be five minutes. Could be not at all." He opened the door. "This is the living area. If somebody calls it'll buzz in here. There's

the kitchen to the right. Oh, and the bathroom is that door on the left."
He pointed to a door across the hallway from the kitchen door.

"Not exactly an open floorplan," she said, laughing.

"It's the 1950s," Hendrix said. "Should have seen the furniture that
was here when I got this job. I replaced a lot of it in the last couple
years."

"You look so worried," Maria said.

"I upset you," he said. "Let's go sit in the living room."

"Okay," Maria said, following him.

He motioned to the couch. "We can sit there."

"Can you hold me for a minute?" she asked, trembling.

"Oh, of course," Hendrix said, taking her into his arms. She
hugged him tight, the tears coming. After a few seconds she was
sobbing. He caressed her back, trying to comfort her, tears welling in
his eyes.

"It's safe here," he whispered. "We're gonna be okay."

She pulled back and looked into his eyes. "Thanks. I was so scared.
We can sit now, as long as you sit next to me."

"Of course," he said. They sat, her turning towards him.

"Can we talk now?" she asked softly.

"Yeah," he said, looking like a child in trouble.

She smiled. "You look like you're about to get slapped. You don't
get what's going on, do you?"

"I went too far tonight," he said. "Especially after you started
feeling the drinks."

"Stop," she said. "I see the real you now. It hit me hard tonight."

He looked at her, heart pounding, not sure what to say.

She sighed. "I think I'm falling for you. Don't you see it?"

"You are?" he asked, eyes tearing up. "Really? Are you sure?"

"Oh, yeah, I'm sure," she said, touching his face.

"Just tonight?" he asked.

"It started yesterday, but I didn't realize it. Then today, when you were looking at me in the office. Oh my God."

"When?" he asked.

"After you told me how much you liked being with me. Remember?"

"Yes," he said quietly.

"Nobody's ever looked at me like that before," she said. "That's when I realized how you feel about me."

"I told you how I felt," Hendrix said.

"Yes, you told me, that day I got mad at you. I thought it was all just lust with you. That look today was different. It shocked me."

"You could tell that I'm in love you," Hendrix said, tears starting down his cheeks.

"Yes," she said. "I didn't see that before, and then tonight happened."

"I didn't mess it up, did I?"

"You really think you're horrible, don't you?" she said.

"Well, I've…"

"Stop." She moved closer and kissed him, gently at first, passion building between them. They broke the kiss and stared in each other's eyes.

"I can't believe it," Hendrix said.

"Neither can I," she said, her breath heaving, eyes full of life and love.

Hendrix stared into her eyes. "So what do we do now?"

"I don't know," she said. "I have a lot of thinking to do. Let's just get through tonight, okay?"

A buzzer went off.

"Somebody's here," Hendrix said. He got up. "C'mon, let's go back to the console and see who it is."

"You want me to hide somewhere?" she asked. "You know, so everybody doesn't know."

"No way," Hendrix said. "I don't care who knows. You don't, do you?"

"No," she said, her arm going around his waist as they walked to the console. He looked at the video.

"It's Holly and Chief Ramsey." Hendrix chuckled. "There's a pair." He hit a button and the gate opened. They drove inside, parking next to the garage door.

"Why don't you go get the TV turned on in the living room, and put it on a news channel. I'll let them in."

"Sure," she said, reaching up to kiss him one more time. She turned to leave.

"I could get used to that," he said, smiling at her. She turned back and gave him a coy smile. He pushed the garage door opener button and watched as it rolled up. Holly and Chief Ramsey rushed in.

"Close that right now," Ramsey shouted. Hendrix nodded and hit the button again, before the door had opened all the way. They watched it come down, then rushed in.

"You guys okay?" Hendrix asked.

"Lock the big door," Ramsey said. "All the gates around the perimeter secured?"

"Yeah," Hendrix said. "You guys look terrified."

"Mr. Hendrix, the news is on," Maria said. "You better check this out."

"Maria's here?" Holly asked.

"Yeah," Hendrix said. "We were having dinner about a block away from where the tanks started shooting."

"My God," Ramsey said, watching the big vault door close.

"Why so worried? I saw the jets start blowing up tanks before we got here."

"Mr. Hendrix!" Maria called.

"Coming," he said, leading the men inside. "What is it?"

"It's not just tanks," she said, horrified look on her face. "There's troops. A lot of troops."

"That's what we're worried about," Ramsey said. "We estimate that about twenty thousand troops have entered the city from the south so far. We've knocked out about half the tanks, but we can't take out the men without troops of our own."

"State and city officials have been ordered into their secure locations," Holly said. "This is going to be a siege."

"Oh no," Maria said, eyes wide.

"This facility will be used as one of the communications hubs," Ramsey said. "Glad to see you have Maria here. You know the protocol, don't you, Maria?"

"Yes sir," Maria said. "I haven't had to use it, but I've had the training."

"Good," Ramsey said.

"Are we expecting others here tonight?" Hendrix asked.

"Doubtful, and we'll have to leave soon," Holly said. "We're making the rounds before the troops can get this far north. At the rate they were moving, they'll hold the southern part of the city in short order."

"They can do that with twenty thousand men?" Hendrix asked.

"That's not all they have. There's another eighty-thousand or so on the way here, coming up I-35."

"Oh my God," Maria said, her hand going to her mouth.

"Yeah, what she said," Holly cracked. "We've got to go. Lock up right after, and stay down here. Both of you."

"Okay," Hendrix said, walking them out. "How many more locations are open?"

"Six on this side of town. More around the Capitol. Some in the medical district to the east, and up around Round Rock."

"Where's Nelson?" Hendrix asked. "He okay?"

"He's safe," Ramsey said. "He's with Gallagher and Landry right now. Can't say where."

"Anything going on in the other large cities?"

"We don't know," Holly said. "We've lost communications with the leadership in San Antonio and Dallas. Houston appears to be okay, after we locked it down a few days ago."

"This is an all-out war now," Ramsey said. "This system buzzes you wherever you are down here, right?"

"Yes," Hendrix said. "Even if I fall asleep, it'll shock me awake. It's loud."

"Okay, we're out of here," Ramsey said. "If you get a call from another one of the secure locations, have Maria use the protocol. We don't want the enemy knowing where the locations are."

"Understood," Maria said. "I'll be ready."

"Good," Ramsey said. "Like I said, it's good that you're here. See you two later, hopefully."

"Take care," Hendrix said. He walked them to the back and let them out of the garage, then rushed to the console and watched as they approached the front gate, opening it, then shutting it as soon as they got through. He turned to Maria.

"I'm so scared," she said, rushing over to him.

"We'll be okay in here," he said. He turned a key by the vault door and the big bolts around it moved out with a clunk. "We could have troops all over the compound and they won't be getting in here."

"What if they cut the power?"

"The generator will kick in, and it's in here so they can't get to it. Let's go see what's going on."

She nodded and followed him into the living room, sitting with him on the couch. The commentators were struggling to have enough to say with no video feed.

"How long can we stay in here?" Maria asked.

"There's enough food and water for several months," Hendrix said. "Might get tired of some of the food."

"I don't have any clothes other than this," she said.

"That's the least of our worries," Hendrix said, smiling, trying to lighten things. She smiled and shook her head.

"That's naughty. Maybe you have some things I can wear."

"Sure," he said," I've got some over-sized t-shirts that you could wear. Probably some gym shorts and sweats that you could wear in a pinch. It'll be okay. We won't be stuck down here forever."

"There's probably laundry machines too, I'll bet."

"Yes, as a matter of fact," Hendrix said.

"Good," she said. "I doubt if you have any bras laying around here."

"Another thing that doesn't bother me," Hendrix said. "Sorry. I'll knock it off."

"Don't be afraid," she said. "I'm not going to be that way with you anymore."

The system buzzed at them.

"Time to go to work," Hendrix said. They got off the couch and rushed to the console.

"You take it," Hendrix said.

She nodded and got on, navigating to the emergency communications window. "Go ahead, please."

"Ramsey here, Maria. We need to send an unlock message to sector 25488, facility 65849."

"What's that?" Hendrix asked.

"Armory," Ramsey said. "We've got about seven hundred civilians there who need something better than hunting rifles to fight with."

"Good," Hendrix said. "We're going to need this kind of help."

Ramsey chuckled. "Look at us, on the same side for once."

"Yeah, Texas needs us to focus," Hendrix said. "Maria just sent the message."

"Excellent," Ramsey said. "Thanks."

"You someplace safe?"

"Not yet, Kip, but don't worry about us. Thanks."

The line went dead.

"Wow, seven hundred, eh," Maria said, looking up at him.

"There will be more," Hendrix said. "Hope there's some leader types among them. Like those folks who were at the Austin attack when this was getting started."

"Those rednecks?" Maria asked.

"Yeah, those rednecks," Hendrix said. "Wonder where they are."

"In hiding with the Austin cops who were involved with them at the Superstore, according to the news last week," Maria said.

"Well, hopefully they won't stay in hiding for too long. We're gonna need people like them."

"You look exhausted," Maria said.

"Been a long night," Hendrix said. "Glad I didn't drink a third martini."

"That seems like so long ago," she said as they walked back into the living room. "Where do we sleep?"

"See that door over there?" he asked, pointing to the far left corner of the room.

"Yeah," she said.

"There's twelve bedrooms back there, with communications consoles and video monitor screens. The laundry and additional bathrooms are back there too.

"Where's all the food?" she asked.

"The door at the far end of the kitchen," Hendrix said. "There's a walk-in freezer and fridge, a big pantry, and water tanks there. The generator is also in that area."

"Wow, this is the hot doomsday spot then, isn't it?"

Hendrix chuckled. "Yeah, like I said, I used to think it was overkill. Not so much now." He yawned.

"The buzzers go off everywhere, though, right? Even in the bedrooms?"

"Yeah," Hendrix said.

"Good," she said. "Show me."

"Sure," he said, leading her to the door. They went through, into a long hallway with doors on either side and exposed plumbing running along the ceiling, fire sprinklers every four feet. "Not very glamorous."

"Looks like something out of a sci-fi movie," Maria said. "Where's the laundry?"

"That first door on the right," Hendrix said, opening it.

"Wow, there's five sets of machines in there."

"This is designed for about thirty people," Hendrix said.

"Really?" she asked.

"Might get a little close in here with that many," Hendrix said.

"Well, let's see how the bedrooms are," Maria said.

Hendrix led her to the first door on the other side of the hallway, opening it and standing aside for her. "This is the leader's quarters. The rest are more like barracks, with bunk beds."

"This isn't bad," she said, looking around the room as Hendrix went to the bedside table and switched on a lamp. There was a queen-sized bed in the middle of the room, along with dressers, a console, a TV, and a private bathroom.

"It's pretty nice," Hendrix said, looking around. "Gets a little cold down here at night."

"You've slept in here before?"

"Only for drills," Hendrix said. "Another thing I used to think was silly."

She smiled at him, then went to the door and closed it. "I think we need a little quiet time. She turned to him, then pulled her sweater over her head, tossing it aside, showing her white lace bra.

"Oh, geez," Hendrix said, staring at her. "What are you doing?"

"So many questions," she said as her hands went behind her back, undoing the bra. She pulled it off, her full breasts bouncing into view. "Here's what you wanted. She walked towards him, her arms going around him as they kissed passionately, Hendrix not sure how aggressive he should be, tentatively moving his hands on her bare back. She broke the kiss and put his hands on her breasts, moaning as he touched them.

"Oh, Maria," he said. "I love you so." It was like a dam bursting after that, both of them removing the rest of their clothes frantically, falling on the bed together, their passion for each other white-hot. Maria was beside herself as he took her, trembling and bucking and crying out over and over.

They lay spent afterwards, next to each other on their backs, their breathing slowing. Maria looked at him. "Well, that worked."

Hendrix chuckled. "What do you mean?"

"Us," she said, turning on her side towards him. "We work. That doesn't always happen, you know. Even if the affection is there."

He pulled her close, kissing her deeply as she put her leg over his hip, his hands roving all over, melding with her, owning her. She pulled back and looked at him again, eyes tearing up, trembling.

"Second thoughts?" he asked.

"Will you stop with that?" she asked. "That's not what I was thinking. Not even close."

"What then?"

"Love," she said. "Happiness. Life. Us together."

"You really think you could love me?"

"I think I do love you," she said, then paused. "No, I don't think."

"Oh, God yes," he said, pulling her in for another kiss. She pulled back afterward.

"You're ready again," she said.

"Are you?" he asked. She rolled on top of him, taking him inside again, biting her lower lip, not able to speak, eyes locked on his.

They woke later, the buzzer going off again.

{ 20 }

Resistance

Kelly sat in front of the TV set in the clubhouse, eyes wide and staring at the screen, next to Nate, Junior, Gray, Moe, Clancy, and Fritz. Rachel and Brenda walked in out of the darkness.

"Can you believe this?" Rachel asked. "They're strong enough to hit a city like Austin?"

"The look on your face scares me," Brenda said, getting next to Kelly.

"I want to go hit them so bad I can taste it," Kelly said.

"Me too," Junior said. "Wonder what's the best way for us to approach?"

"Hold it," Brenda said. "No. You'll just get killed."

"We need to be part of a bigger force if we're going in there," Kelly said to Junior. "Brenda's right about that. We'll just get ourselves killed if we go in there on our own."

"What about Curt's toys?" Fritz asked.

"And our tanks?" Gray asked.

"Won't be enough," Kelly said. "We need to go hit the henhouse while the roosters are away."

"What do you mean, exactly?" Fritz asked.

"I know what he means," Junior said. "These guys have limited resources. We need to do what all resistance fighters do. Find their stockpiles and destroy them. Take away their safe havens. Figure out how to expose their locations and supply chains to the forces who can do something about them."

"We can also organize others to build a force," Nate said.

"Damn straight we can, and we will," Junior said, "but that will take time. Meanwhile we need to survive. Chip away at them. Create havoc. Throw monkey wrenches."

"Exactly," Kelly said. "Look, I'm plenty pissed off at these guys. My initial reaction is to go kick some ass. That's not always the best play. Last I looked we didn't have a hundred thousand men, all with military equipment. We have a rag-tag force of irregulars with an odd assortment of weapons. Yeah, we have a genius in our midst who can give us an edge – and that will work for some things, but it won't hold back a flood of well-equipped enemy fighters."

"Great, now I'm slightly less scared than I was a minute ago," Brenda said.

"I get what he's saying," Rachel said. "We need to be using our noggins. I heard Curt talking about the phones. Maybe we ought to talk to him. Maybe he can figure out where the enemy bases are. Then we hit them and escape like a thief in the night."

"I like the way you're thinking," Junior said, smiling at her. "Knew you were a smarty-pants."

"I think he likes you," Brenda whispered to Rachel. She giggled.

"Stop it," she whispered back.

"I'm gonna go talk to Curt right now," Junior said.

"I'll go with you," Kelly said.

"Think I'll stay here for a while if you don't mind," Brenda said.

"Me too," Rachel said.

Kelly and Junior headed out the door.

"You getting sweet on Rachel, Junior?" Kelly asked.

"I just love her to death, but I know that's not gonna happen," he said. "Don't worry, I'm not going to get myself hurt, and I'm not going to make her feel bad either."

"Glad to hear it," Kelly said. "We'll be lucky if we survive this war. You know that, right?"

"We're smarter than you think," Junior said, flashing him a silly grin. "Who's worried about a couple old codgers like us? We can use that."

Kelly laughed. "We're not that old."

"Don't tell them that," Junior said. "What the hell is Curt doing up there?"

Curt was on the roof of his toy-hauler garage with a big drill, wearing safety glasses and a head-mounted LED light.

"Curt!" Kelly shouted, trying to get above the drilling noise.

He looked down and then shut off the drill, taking off the safety glasses and removing his ear plugs. "What's up, guys?"

"What the hell are you doing?" Kelly asked.

"I'm putting that other remote-control machine gun up here," he said. "To guard my rear."

"You've got to be kidding me," Junior said, laughing. "That gonna work?"

"You doubt me?" he asked as he climbed down on the ladder.

"I don't," Kelly said. "Got a question. You think you can still tune in on enemy phones? We want to find the base for the ones who just attacked Austin."

"Austin?" Curt asked, shocked look on his face.

"Shit, he don't know," Junior said, looking at Kelly.

"Well, it did just happen, and he's been busy," Kelly said. He looked at Curt. "The enemy took a bunch of tanks and about twenty thousand men into Austin tonight, from the south. They're working their way towards the city center."

"Oh, shit," Curt said, sitting down. "You want to go join the fight?"

"Nah, there's too many of them," Kelly said. "We want to know where they've got their supplies."

Curt got a grin on his face. "Now there's a good idea. They've probably got a bunch of tank fuel and ammo. Imagine what I could do to it with the Barracuda."

"That's the direction we were thinking in," Junior said.

"I'll start working on that," Curt said, taking off the LED light off of his head. "I've got three different phones with numbers loaded. I'll start looking at them with my program. Maybe I can find a cluster of them south of Austin."

"That would be great," Kelly said. "Thanks."

"I'll get back with you," he said, climbing into his garage. He opened a cabinet and took out a covered pan. "I'll have to charge these up a little bit. Batteries on all of them are dead now. Take me a little while to do that and search. I'll get back to what I was working on while they charge. Okay?"

"Okay, fair enough," Junior said. "Thanks!"

"Yeah, thanks," Kelly said. "We'll go back to the girls and keep tabs of the news. Call me if you need me."

Curt nodded, and they walked away.

"He's our ace in the hole," Kelly said. "Could you imagine if we can pull this off?"

"It'll renew the target on our backs."

"True," Kelly said. "The enemy will get wise, too. They'll dump their phones."

"So the trick is to do enough damage before they figure it out."

"You got it," Kelly said as they walked back into the clubhouse. Everybody turned to them. "Anything happen?"

"Jets took out some of the tanks, but there's a lot more enemy fighters flooding in," Fritz said. "Citizens are starting to fight back, at least."

"Good," Junior said.

"You okay?" Kelly asked, looking at Brenda's terrified face.

"No, I'm not okay," she said. "They had video up again for a few minutes. It's gone again, but you should have seen all the enemy fighters rushing around. They move fast, and they were killing everybody they ran up against."

"I'm scared," Rachel said, hugging Junior. She sobbed onto his shoulder.

"Lucky Junior," Fritz said.

"Shut up," Rachel said. "He's my friend."

"Yes, you are, sweet pea," Junior said, patting her back. "I'm always here for you."

"What are we going to do if a force that size rushes in here?" Brenda asked.

"Die," Kelly said. "That's why Kyle, Jason, and I were talking about it earlier. This park isn't very defensible. The only advantage we have is the long sightline we have with the tanks."

"They have tanks," Brenda said.

"I know," Kelly said. "We'll have to head for someplace a little more remote."

"Hey, turn up the sound," Fritz said, looking at the TV. "Something's happening."

Moe picked up the remote and raised the volume.

"Citizens gained access to the National Guard Armory earlier and weapons have been distributed to a growing number of Texas Patriots," the commentator said, barely able to hold back her smile. "The group started seven-hundred strong, but several hundred more have arrived since then, and more are streaming in as we speak. They are lining South Congress Avenue, on roof tops and in windows, pouring fire down on the approaching fighters. Mortars have been set up along 11th Street, and have begun firing white phosphorus anti-personnel rounds. It's estimated that several thousand enemy fighters have died from the counter-attack so far. There was a brief outcry by some of the people milling around the Capitol building about the use of white phosphorus, but angry citizens beat them and chased them away."

"Some idiots never learn," Fritz said.

"You've been awful quiet, Moe," Kelly said.

"I'll have to leave my place," he said. "The handwriting's on the wall. Kinda like the place. I'm not happy about it."

"I know," Kelly said quietly. "No way we can stay here. We need to get tires for those flatbeds tomorrow, and get ready to high-tail it. You are going with us, right?"

"If you'll have me," he said quietly.

"Are you kidding?" Kelly said, putting his arm on his shoulder. "You're one of us, and you gave us a great port in the storm for a little while. You'll get your place back after this is over."

"Hope so," he said. "I know of several other locations we might consider. I'll start looking into them in a little more detail."

"Good, you do that," Kelly said. "You got a rig?"

"Big pusher," he said. "Clancy's got a rig too. Maybe I ought to get the batteries charged up tonight."

"We probably won't have to leave that quickly," Kelly said.

"Look at how many men they have," Moe said. "I'm betting they know we hit their tank hijacking. We'll be lucky if they don't end up here before end of the day tomorrow."

"I think we have a little more time that that," Kelly said. "Maybe I just hope we do. Doesn't hurt to be ready."

"I think we should start stowing stuff first thing in the morning, Kelly," Brenda said.

"We have a stalemate on South Congress Avenue," the commentator said. "The mortar rounds stopped the advance towards the Capitol, so the enemy left a force there to return fire, while attempting to move the remainder of their force to the west. The citizens are pursuing them, both sides taking many casualties. Apache attack helicopters are in the south part of the city, attempting to stop the flow of enemy fighters coming up I-35, with mixed results. Several Apaches have been shot down with hand-held missile launchers."

"Oh, geez," Brenda said.

"Don't lose hope," Kelly said. "We've got only a thousand people right there. There's a lot more where that came from."

"He's right," Clancy said, looking at his iPad. "Guess how many gun owners there are in Texas."

"Few hundred thousand?" Rachel asked.

Clancy laughed. "Almost ten million."

"Holy shit," Rachel said.

"Yeah, this ain't over," Kelly said. "Not by a long shot."

"But how many are military grade?" Moe asked.

"Enough," Kelly said, "but with those kind of numbers, it really doesn't matter that much. Ten million single-shot rifles would be hard to beat by any army in the world. It's just basic math."

"Yeah, he's right," Clancy said. "Once this really starts going, Islamist body disposal will become a problem."

"All body disposal will become a problem," Kelly said. "Lots of good Texans are gonna get killed. This won't be a turkey shoot. It's going to be a big mess for everybody involved, and each and every one of us stands to lose somebody we love. I'd keep that in mind."

"Oh, God," Brenda said. "I didn't really get that before."

"I knew it, but nothing brings reality home like seeing tanks rolling into Austin," Junior said. "We have to win this. We have to stay strong."

Curt ran into the room. "Guess what I found?" he asked.

Kelly and Junior looked at each other and grinned.

"Uh oh," Brenda said.

Curt held up the enemy phone, and the men gathered around.

"There's a big group of them in the woods north of Mountain City," he said. "I'll bet they've got all kinds of supplies there. Ready for a road trip?"

"Shit, man, that's five hours away, assuming we can stay on I-10 most of the way," Moe said.

"So we tow the Barracuda with Jason's jeep," Junior said. "Take Kyle's truck."

"You got the fifty-cal working?" Clancy asked. "Bitchen."

"What about the tanks?"

"Somebody's got to protect the homestead," Junior said. "Besides, we'd just lose them there. They've probably got their reserve tanks at that location. We can outrun them with the Barracuda, Jeeps, and Kyle's truck. Can't with a tank."

"Exactly," Kyle said.

"I'll go get my bikers," Gray said. "We'll haul ass down there and reconnoiter. We can leave in about five minutes."

"Yeah, you do that," Curt said. "I'd better go get Jason and Kyle up."

"Count us in," Junior said.

"Yeah, Kelly said. "We're going to need to drive shifts."

"Yep," Junior said.

Brenda looked at Kelly. "No way I can talk you out of this, is there?"

"No," Kelly said.

"Okay," she said. "I don't like it, but I hitched myself to a man. Probably be disappointed if you chickened out."

Kelly took her into his arms and kissed her passionately, then looked her in the eyes. "You might have to fight. Be ready."

"Understand," she said.

"Let's go," Kelly shouted.

{ 21 }

Biology

Jason laid on his back in the dark bedroom, not able to sleep. Carrie was still out in the salon watching TV. He heard a knock on the door. Dingo growled.

"Jason?" Carrie said. "You still up? Curt's outside."

"Coming," Jason said, getting out of bed and getting into his pants. "What's wrong?" he asked when he saw Carrie's face.

"Tanks and a lot of enemy troops are attacking Austin up I-35."

"No shit?" Jason said, heading for the door. He opened it. Curt came in.

"You see what's going on?" Curt asked.

"Just now," Jason said. "We don't have the resources to counter-attack."

"You're right," Curt said, "but there is something we can do. We need to take off now, while they're busy."

"Dammit," Carrie said.

"You don't know what he's asking for yet," Jason said softly. "What do you have in mind?"

"I used their cellphones to figure out where their base is."

"Where?" Jason asked.

"Mountain City," he said.

"Shit, that's four or five hours away," Carrie said. "More with the RVs."

"It's just under five hours," Curt said.

"What do you want to do?" Jason asked.

"Sneak in the back and blow up whatever tank fuel and ammo we can find," Curt said. "Kelly's talking to Kyle about it right now. Some of Gray's bikers just took off to reconnoiter."

"I don't like this," Carrie said.

"Neither do I, honey, but we need to do this. What do you have in mind, Curt?"

"Tow the Barracuda behind your Jeep again. Take Kyle's truck. Enough people so we can drive continuously through the night. It'll still be dark when we get there if we leave now."

"How come the Apaches haven't found them?" Carrie asked.

"They're in the hills above Mountain City. Lots of tree cover there," Curt said. "Besides, those Apaches are a little busy right now."

"I'll go get dressed," Jason said.

"Good, I'll pull the Barracuda behind your Jeep." He left the coach as Jason went into the bedroom. Carrie followed him back there.

"You can't talk me out of this," he said.

"I know," she said, hugging him. "I don't have to like it. Wonder how Kate is taking it?"

"She'll probably want to go," Jason said.

"So do I," Carrie said.

"You're pregnant, and you have our daughter to take care of."

"I know, honey," Carrie said. "You'd better not get killed."

"I won't," he said. "We'll strike and get the hell out of there."

"You're going to drive all the way back here afterwards?"

"Maybe," Jason said. "Or maybe we'll rest at the folk's house. Eric is there right now, remember."

"Okay," she said. "It's probably safer than here. That thin road in the hills is a good choke point."

"Yeah, I told Eric we might end up there," Jason said. "It's quite a few acres." He finished dressing and went for the door, Carrie following him. Kate was outside watching Kyle load the mounted .50 cal. She was crying. Carrie walked over to her.

"You okay?" Carrie asked.

"No, but I know it has to happen," she said.

"You going?"

"I wanted to, but he talked me out of it," she said. "I'm going to make a deal with one of Gray's people to pull the trailer if we have to leave before they can get back."

"Shit, I didn't think about that," Carrie said. "I'll have to drive this beast."

"You can do it," Kate said.

"Hey, Kyle," Jason said, "I'll set one of the BARs and ammo on the floor in your cab, okay?"

"Yeah, buddy, thanks," Kyle said. "Junior's going to ride with me, so I might have to stash it behind the seat."

"I'll go with you, if you don't mind," Kelly said, walking up, Brenda next to him.

"Sure," Jason said. "Glad to have you."

"How are you feeling about this?" Brenda asked Kate and Carrie.

"How do you think?" Carrie asked.

"Yeah, what she said," Kate said. "You?"

"I don't like it, but it's the man I chose," she said. "I think Rachel is taking this as bad as I am." She nodded. Rachel was close to Junior, talking to him, arms waving around.

"Don't worry, Rachel," Junior said. "I'll be fine. Really."

"You better not get killed," she said, hugging him, turning her head up to kiss him. He thought it was going to be on the cheek, but she kissed him on the mouth.

"You don't like me that way," Junior said.

"I want you back here," she whispered. "You make it back, and I'll give you a good roll in the hay."

Juniors eyes got wider and he chuckled. "No you won't, but the thought will be nice on the long drive."

"You might be surprised," she said.

"I wouldn't risk ruining our friendship, and that's the truth," he said, stroking her hair. "You're gonna have to drive the Brave if something happens before we get back. You know where the keys are, right?"

"Yeah," she said, looking up at his face again.

"Hey, Junior, while we're young," Kelly called to him. Then he climbed into the passenger seat of the Jeep.

"Coming," he said, rushing to Kyle's truck.

Curt finished hitching the Barracuda, and rushed to the back seat, behind Jason. "Let's go, man," he said. Jason nodded and drove ahead, Kyle following him with Junior.

Rachel walked over to the other women. They watched their men leave silently.

"There they go," Rachel said, sniffling.

"What were you talking to Junior about over there?" Brenda asked.

Rachel giggled, wiping the tears away from her eyes. "I told the old coot I'd screw him if he came back okay."

"You didn't," Brenda said, then started laughing. "That'll give him some incentive."

"He said he wouldn't," she said. "Doesn't want to ruin what we have."

"He's a lot smarter than he appears," Kate said. "I've really gotten to like him."

"I know, me too," Carrie said, "and Chelsea just loves him."

"You wouldn't really, would you?" Brenda asked. "It's not like you love him."

"I do love him, but not like that," Rachel said.

"Then why would you even consider it?" Kate asked.

"Because men like him are vital now," Rachel said, determination on her face. "We need to keep our society together, and a lot of that is on us women. So yeah, I'd screw him. Hell, I'd have his baby."

"You're serious, aren't you?" Brenda asked.

"Deadly serious," she said. "You picked a good man. From what I heard, everybody was surprised."

"Oh, I had a huge crush on him for quite a while," Brenda said, "but I didn't let him know about it. It's different, though."

"Why?" Rachel asked.

"Well, for one thing, he's about two years older than me," she said. "You know how old Junior is, right?"

"Yes, he's sixteen years older than me," she said. "Like I said, I don't love him that way, but the age difference wouldn't stop me. Look at Hollywood. This age difference seems to be the norm there."

Carrie giggled. "Yeah, you've got a point."

"I'm going to try to get some sleep," Carrie said. "Chelsea will be up bright and early. Talk to you tomorrow."

The others nodded as she climbed into her rig.

"She's so strong," Rachel said. "Pregnant with a young child in this world, and she keeps it all together."

Kate snickered. "Kyle and I are trying."

"You're joking," Brenda said. "Now? Really?"

"The urge is incredible," Kate said.

"You two going to get married?" Rachel asked.

"I already consider us married," she said. "We'll officially tie the knot before too long. We've already talked about it."

"He worships the ground you walk on, that's for sure," Brenda said.

"As Kelly does with you," Kate said.

Brenda was quiet for a minute, eyes tearing up. "Hell, if I could, I'd let Kelly knock me up too, probably. I've had the urges, even with my plumbing all messed up."

"Hysterectomy?" Rachel asked.

"Yeah," she said, "six years ago. I'd probably be done by now anyway."

"How about you, Rachel?" Kate asked. "Your plumbing still work?"

Rachel looked at her and smiled. "Oh, I think everything still works. Had a baby, but it died." She started to tear up.

"Oh no, what happened?" Kate asked.

"SIDS," she said. "On a camping trip with my first husband. I went off the deep end after that. Lost the marriage and pretty much everything else."

"How long ago?" Brenda asked.

"Ten years," she said. "I do have the urge to get pregnant too, though. I can't understand it."

"It's the times," Kate said. "The struggle. I read about that someplace."

"How strong do you have it?" Brenda asked. "Strong enough for Junior?"

She thought about it for a moment. "Shit. Yeah. That's probably what's going on."

"Biology," Kate said. Rachel looked at her and flashed a wicked grin.

"Junior ain't gonna know what hit him when he gets back."

Brenda giggled. "No way."

"Yes way," she said. "I just decided. I'm gonna screw his brains out until it works."

"What if he doesn't work?" Kate asked.

"Oh, he works," she said. "Hard not to notice. We have been living together in that little motor home, after all. He likes to look at me. He thinks I don't notice."

The three of them giggled, but then their faces got serious.

"I hope they make it back," Brenda said, tears running down her face.

Kate and Rachel nodded, and they all went back to their rigs.

{ 22 }

Waiting

Lita sat behind the bar in the dim light. There was a soft knock on the door. She looked at her phone. Almost 2:00 AM. Another soft knock.

"Coming," she said as she walked to the door. She looked out the window and opened it, letting Hannah and Madison in.

"Hi, Lita," Madison said, brushing her blonde hair back. "Hear anything yet?"

"They won't be here for a while," Lita said. "They have to put the boat away and drive over here."

"Did you see that fireball to the north?" Hannah asked, taking off her coat.

"Heard about it on the news," Lita said. "Sea plane trying to rush in under the radar. I suspect our men had something to do with it."

"Our men?" Hannah asked, smiling.

"Yeah, you're serious about Richardson, but the two of us just met ours," Madison said.

"You like them," Lita said. "I can tell. And here you are in the middle of the night."

"Okay, I do have a strong attraction for Brendan," Hannah said. "Makes me tingle when I think about him."

"Tingle?" Madison asked. "Oh brother."

"You don't have any reaction to Juan Carlos?" Hannah asked. "You two were hot and heavy last night, as I remember."

"Oh, I have the usual biological reactions," she said. "Not to be crude."

Lita and Hannah looked at her and laughed.

"Typical Madison comment," Hannah said. "TMI, by the way."

"So sue me," she said. "How long are they going to be here?"

Lita shrugged. "Why ask me?"

"C'mon, your boyfriend is the leader, right?" Madison asked.

"He's only a lieutenant," she said. "He told me he didn't know. Could be weeks. Could be days."

"You trying to figure out if you should get serious or not?" Hannah asked.

"Of course, aren't you?" Madison asked.

"I'm just letting my emotions guide me," Hannah said. "Seeing where it leads. We've gotten thrown together. I'm liking it so far."

"Would you have let Brendan pick you up, if you just saw him in a bar?" Lita asked.

Hannah thought about it for a second. "You know, I probably would have gone for Juan Carlos first, just based on looks."

"Why didn't you?" Madison asked. "I didn't pick him before you got a chance. It was the other way around. I remember when you two locked eyes."

"Would you have gone after him instead?" Hannah asked.

"He's too much the sensitive type for me," Madison said, "but let's be honest. They're both hot. Either one of us would have been interested in either one of them under normal circumstances."

Hannah giggled. "Yeah, you're probably right."

"I think they're coming," Lita said, listening. "I hope it's them, anyway."

There was a rap on the door. Lita rushed over and looked. "It's them all right." She opened the door and stood aside.

"What's that thing?" Madison asked.

"SMAW," Richardson said. "We brought it with us from the boat." He sat it down on the bar with a box of ammo.

"That looks like a bazooka," Hannah said.

"You guys have guns with you this time, too," Lita said. "Should we be worried?"

"You hear what happened earlier?" Richardson asked.

"The plane," Lita said. "Yeah. Was that you?"

"Yep," Juan Carlos said.

"Why do you look so worried," Madison asked, walking next to him. "What happened?"

"That plane had a nuke on board," Brendan whispered.

"Don't spread that around," Richardson said quickly. "They'll throw us in the brig if they know we said anything."

"We won't," Hannah said, fear in her eyes.

"Shit, you think there may be another one you have to shoot down," Lita said.

"Chances are slim, but you never know," Richardson said. "We have a good vantage point here. Figured it wouldn't hurt to bring it."

"So you guys are going to spend the whole night watching the sky?" Madison asked.

"Madison, you know what just about happened," Hannah said. "That could have killed all of us." Brendan pulled her close and caressed her head as she trembled.

"They weren't going to blow it here," Richardson said. "They were taking it somewhere with more people. Corpus Christi, or closer to Houston."

"So why was it flying close to us?" Lita asked, putting her arm around Richardson's waist.

"If they went out over the open Gulf, one of those Coast Guard cutters would have shot them down. If they went over the land, they'd have to fight off anti-aircraft guns and probably planes too. They figured they could slip through the bay area un-noticed."

"They were mistaken," Juan Carlos said. "Man, I love that M-19."

"What's a M-19?" Madison asked. She came over to Juan Carlos and sat on his lap. He kissed her, but she broke it. "No, really, what is it?"

"It's an automatic grenade launcher," Juan Carlos said. "Fires as fast as I can pull the trigger. It's mounted on the boat."

"Wow," Madison said. "That sounds hot."

"Oh, yeah, baby," he said, "but not has hot as you. Come here."

"I'm already on your lap," she said. He pulled her face to his and kissed her deeply. She resisted at first, but then moaned into him.

"That looks like fun," Hannah said, pulling Brendan close to her and kissing him.

"Kids," Richardson said, following Lita behind the bar. She turned and threw her arms around him, kissing him passionately. Then she looked him in the eyes. "I love you so much. I was scared the whole time you were out there."

"I know," he said. "I love you too. Wish this was over."

"Any idea how long you'll be around here?"

"The brass isn't saying anything," he said. "Let's just enjoy it while we can."

"It's hard," she said, resting her head against his chest.

"I know, sweetie." They hugged silently, watching the younger couples making out.

"Wow," Lita whispered. "Maybe we should be somewhere that they can have a little privacy."

"We don't want to go there," Richardson whispered. "At least not yet. I wanted them to blow off steam. We don't want them too serious. Not now."

"We're serious," Lita whispered.

"True, but we were serious a couple years before any of this started."

Suddenly there was a noise outside, approaching from the south.

"Hey," Richardson said. "Sound like a prop plane to you?"

"Dammit," Juan Carlos said. "Yeah, it does."

"Yep," Brendan said. "Let's get out there now."

"You want to go on the roof?" Lita asked. "It's got some cover. You can get up there through the stock room."

"Good idea," Richardson said, picking up the SMAW. "C'mon, you guys. Girls, stay away from the windows, okay? That seaplane we splashed had guns."

"C'mon, girls," Lita said, leading them into the kitchen as the men rushed to the stock room.

"Wish we had a .50 cal," Brendan said as they went up the ladder. Richardson opened the trap door and they got onto the roof.

"It's close," Juan Carlos said.

"Who's best with this thing?" Richardson asked.

"Brendan," Juan Carlos said.

"Okay," Richardson said. "You help him reload. I'm gonna call it in. Hopefully those choppers can be here in a hurry." He pulled out his cellphone and called as Brendon set up the SMAW.

"Hand me a rocket," Brendan said. Juan Carlos fished one out of the box and handed it to him. "Have the next one ready." He inserted it into the launcher and held it up, aiming at the sky.

"Where is it, dude?" Juan Carlos asked.

"Can't see it yet," Brendan said. "Damn fog."

"Choppers are close by," Richardson said. "If we don't hit it, they'll take it down."

"What if they decide to set off the device?" Juan Carlos asked.

"We'll all be par-boiled," Richardson said. "Don't worry about it. Do your jobs."

"Roger that, sir," Brendan said. "There it is, look! Another frigging seaplane."

"Lead it," Richardson said.

"The SMAW rockets are faster than the M-19," Juan Carlos said. "Remember that."

"Chopper!" Brendan said, watching it emerge from the fog. It was almost to the seaplane when tracer bullets flashed out of the side door, hitting the chopper, sending it crashing to the water below.

"Dammit!" Brendan shouted. He pulled the trigger, the rocket flying, hitting the side of the plane. It exploded, but the plane kept going.

"Reload," Richardson said.

Brendan had the next round in the launcher before Richardson was done talking.

"Think skeet, dude," Juan Carlos said. "You're good at that."

"Yeah, I am, he said, following the plane. He pulled the trigger. The rocket hit just behind the cockpit, blowing the plane into two pieces.

"Yes!" Brendan shouted as he watched the debris hit the water. Two other choppers showed up and peppered the water around the wreckage with their mini-guns.

"I'll call it in," Richardson said. "Let's leave this thing up here in case there's another one coming."

"Maybe we ought to stay up here," Juan Carlos said.

"Yeah, maybe," Brendan said. "We could let the girls come up, right?"

"Right," Lita said, her head poking through the trap door.

Richardson looked at her, phone to his ear, and nodded yes. She came up, followed by Madison and Hannah.

"You did it, didn't you," Hannah said to Brendan.

"It was a team effort," he said

"What's wrong, honey?" Lita asked, looking at Richardson's face.

"We've got to go now!" he said. "Grab the equipment."

"Why, what's happening?" Lita asked.

"Several Migs and a bunch of Venezuelan attack choppers on the way," Richardson said. "There's going to be an air battle here. We don't want to be around. We need to get inland."

"We can't go over the bridge," Juan Carlos said. "We'd be like sitting ducks on that."

"Seriously," Madison said.

"My dad's fishing boat is right down there," she said. "C'mon."

They rushed down the steps and out the door of the bar, heading for the docks as the sound of choppers approached. Then there was the roar of a jet, and the bar exploded behind them.

"Oh my God!" Hannah cried, looking back at it. Lita was already in the boat, firing up the engine.

"Get in, now!" she cried. The men helped the women in, and Lita took off, racing for the mainland as jets flew at each other and helicopter gunships fought it out above them.

"Where should we land?"

"We can make Port Isabel," Lita said. "Those aircraft are busy with each other now."

There was an explosion to their right, and a big piece of the bridge came down.

"Oh no!" Hannah said, watching cement and vehicles come down onto the water.

"Load the SMAW," Richardson said, watching the skies. "We might not be done fighting."

"Yeah," Brendan said. Juan Carlos handed him another round, and he put it in the launcher and aimed.

"Here comes a chopper."

"You sure it's not one of ours?" Madison asked.

"Yeah, that's Russian," Richardson said.

"We're fighting the Russians?" Hannah asked, eyes wide.

"No, Venezuela has Russian aircraft," Brendan said.

"Better hit them now," Richardson shouted. "If they get any closer, they'll open up on us with their mini-guns."

Brendan squeezed the trigger, the rocket flying into the front of the chopper, blowing it apart. The heat of the blast blanketed them for a moment.

"Reload, dude," Juan Carlos cried, handing Brendan another round. He loaded and aimed again, waiting to see another chopper.

"I don't see any close by," Richardson said.

"We're almost to the harbor," Lita shouted, turning into the long channel.

There were flashes beyond the island, and another Russian chopper fell.

"Good, they got those Coast Guard cutters in place now," Richardson shouted, watching the fireworks above.

Lita pulled into the harbor, taking the first open slip she found.

"Let's get indoors," she said. "My folks place is just down the street."

"They home?"

"No, they left the area," Lita said. "Too dangerous. They tried like hell to get me to leave this morning."

Brendan and Juan Carlos tied the boat up, and they ran off the dock, the jet and chopper noise and explosions still going on.

"How are we going to get back to the patrol boat?" Brendan asked.

"We might be in trouble there," Richardson said.

"You can take my dad's boat over there," Lita said.

"I saw explosions close to those docks," Richardson said. "Our boat might be toast."

"No," Juan Carlos said. "Really?"

"C'mon, man," Brendan said. "We got the precious cargo out of there, and we're alive. I don't care about the damn boat at the moment."

"Am I precious cargo?" Hannah asked, grabbing Brendan's hands as they walked quickly down the street.

"What do you think?" Brendan asked, looking in her eyes.

"There it is," Lita said, out of breath as the made it to the villa. She input a code on the massive gate and it rolled to the side.

"Whoa, dude, look at this joint," Juan Carlos said as they entered the front door. It was ornate marble and wrought iron with art all around, a huge curved staircase in the entry way. They walked past it to the living room.

"You don't think they'll mind?" Brendan asked as they sat.

"No, and frankly, I wouldn't care," she said.

"We aren't out of the woods yet," Richardson said. "This whole area is a target. There a basement in this place?"

"Yeah," Lita said, "Don't know how strong it is, though."

Richardson's phone rang. He answered it.

"It's Jefferson. You guys safe? Put it on speaker."

Richardson put his phone on the coffee table in front of the couch and motioned for the others to gather around. He pushed the speaker button.

"We're at my girlfriend's parents' house in Port Isabel," he said. "With two other women. Don't know about the patrol boat."

"It's gone," Jefferson said. "Our spotters saw the whole dock complex on fire."

"Dammit," Richardson said. "What now?"

"Lie low tonight. Get inland in the morning. Take your women."

"Why?" Lita asked.

"There's about twenty thousand troops heading that way from Matamoros," Jefferson said. "Take route 100 to I-69E. Then take route 2 all the way to Laredo. Wait for instructions there. You have access to a car?"

"There's one in the garage," Lita said. "How do you know the enemy won't get here before morning?"

"They're waiting for armor," Jefferson said. "They ain't gonna get it. We're gonna blow it up tonight. That will slow them down for a while."

"How do you know they're going to come here?" Richardson asked.

"They won't have any place else to go," Jefferson said. "The US Army is coming at them fast from Reynosa."

"The US Army is in Mexico?" Lita asked.

"Long story, but yeah, we've got significant forces there. I've got to go. Be out of there by no later than 8:00 am. Got it?"

"Yes sir," Richardson said. He ended the call.

"You girls okay with this?" Richardson asked.

"I assume you're not talking to me," Lita said.

"No, I'm not talking to you, sweetie," Richardson said.

"I'm going with you guys," Hannah said.

"Me too," Madison said.

"Good," Richardson said. "Let's get some shuteye."

"I'll show you where the bedrooms are," Lita said. "C'mon."

They followed her up the stately curved staircase.

"Separate rooms?" Brendan asked, looking at Hannah.

"Not on your life," she said, putting her arm around his waist as they walked. She was trembling.

Lita and Richardson shot each other a glance, then looked at Madison.

"What?" she asked quickly, looking very agitated. "Of course I'm spending the night with him. So what? I'm scared."

Lita giggled. "I'm not saying a word."

State of the Republic

The buzzing woke Hendrix up right away. Maria's naked body was pressed against him. She stirred, raising her head.

"I need you," Hendrix said. "C'mon, we can use the console in here."

"They'll be able to see us, right?" she asked.

"Yeah, better cover up."

He got out of bed and threw on a robe that was hanging in the closet. Maria pulled the sheet off the bed and wrapped it around herself, groggy as she sat in front of the keyboard. Hendrix switched on the monitor, and she input the codes.

"We're here," Hendrix said. "Who is it?"

"Hi, Kip, it's Nelson."

"Good," Hendrix said. "No video feed?"

"Not from this side. I can see you and your lady friend."

"Maria," Hendrix said.

"Everything okay?" he asked.

"I'm here by choice," Maria said. "Completely."

"It's a good thing she's here," Hendrix said. "She knows the protocol. And yes, we do have a relationship, just so you know."

"I have no problem with that," Nelson said. "Happy for you."

"We have more people coming?"

"No," Nelson said. "Things have gotten a lot worse over the last couple of hours."

"What's going on?"

"We're evacuating most of the Texas state officials out of the city," Nelson said.

"Did they get to the Capitol district yet?"

"No, the citizens stopped them, so they finally gave up and spread out to other places."

"What about the citizens in the rest of Austin?" Hendrix asked.

"General Hogan and General Walker have been organizing around the city, asking the able-bodied fighters to retreat to locations in the burbs. We'll come back in and retake the city soon, but we need leadership for that type of operation. Hogan and Walker are trying to get people with leadership capability up to speed in hours. It's a tall order, but if anybody can pull it off, it's those guys."

"What about the National Guard and the US Army forces who were left in Texas?"

"The US Army still has too many bad apples," Nelson said. "They're bottled up on their bases at the moment, as we investigate everybody."

"How many more tanks are out there?"

"At least fifty," Nelson said. "Could have been a lot worse. We took out the enemy's connections at Fort Bliss, and saved the lion's share of them."

"Why aren't we using the tanks against them, then?"

"Oh, we are," Nelson said. "We're stretched way too thin. That's the real problem. We have battles going on in San Antonio and down around South Padre Island, next to the border. There are enemy troops massing along the New Mexico border. Another group of enemy fighters are collecting close to the east side of Houston. And now we have an armored column heading toward Dallas. We're racing what's left of our tanks to Abilene to cut them off at the pass. We don't want a tank battle in Dallas, that's for sure."

"Dammit," Hendrix said. "What do you want me to do?"

"Stay put for now," Nelson said. "You're one of five secure locations we have left, and you're in a good position to observe. There's the surveillance setup on the roof. You know how to use it, correct?"

"Yes, but you have to be up there to do it," Hendrix said.

"That's a risk we're going to have to take. I need you up there at least once an hour during the daylight to scan the area. Look for tanks and large groups of troops moving around."

"You expecting more to be coming here?"

"No, the enemy is holding the southern half of the town, and it appears they aren't going to go further for the moment. We're worried about them taking off, towards either Waco or San Antonio."

"Oh," Hendrix said. "We aren't using satellites to see this?"

"Feds cut us off," Nelson said. "We've been using planes, but it's risky. We need them for combat, because there are still a lot of Migs south of the border."

"I get it," Hendrix said. "This house is on a bluff. Great view of the entire city."

"Yes," Nelson said. "One thing, though. Try hard not to be seen when you're up there. Pretend there's somebody ready to shoot at you. If you get seen, your compound will get attacked. You can count on that. No lights on in the house at night, either. We're counting on them not knowing the house is occupied."

"Don't they know that this is the residence of the President Pro Tempore?" Maria asked.

"It's not common knowledge, but it's not a secret either," Nelson said. "You could have somebody showing up just because they know it's the residence of a high-ranking official."

"What if somebody shows up?" Hendrix asked. "They could climb the wall and get into the house pretty easily."

"They can't get into the bunker, so if somebody shows, stay in the bunker and pretend you aren't there. During the day, carry a gun with you when you're going to the roof, and make sure you check all the video cameras before going up there. Got it?"

"Yeah," Hendrix said.

"Good," Nelson said. "Talk to you later."

"Wait a minute," Maria said. "My sister is at the medical facility next to the capitol. Is she safe?"

"Yes, Maria, all of the patients and staff there have been moved to other locations," Nelson said. "Don't worry about her."

"Thank you, sir," Maria said.

"Anything else?" Nelson asked.

"Yeah," Hendrix said. "Take care of you yourself."

Nelson chuckled. "You too, old friend."

Nelson ended the call. Hendrix and Maria sat looking at the screen for a moment, their minds racing.

"We could lose Texas," Maria said.

"Yes, we could, but we won't," Hendrix said. "Texans can be infuriating at times. Lord knows I've had problems with them, given my political views. That being said, they aren't easily pushed around, and they love their state more than outsiders understand."

"Is that going to be enough?" Maria asked, turning to Hendrix, clutching him and pulling him closer.

"Anybody who counts out Texas had better get ready."

"Ready for what?" Maria asked.

"Fury."

To be continued in Bug Out! Texas Book 4

Cast Of Characters

Texas Hill Country Group

Jason – Austin PD. Young man with family. Brave, trustworthy, great in a fight, loyal. Six foot four and handsome with thick sable hair. Considered to be a high-potential employee by Austin PD. Responsible. Mid 30s.

Carrie – Jason's wife. Strong, brave, witty, smart. Short dark hair and delicate, pretty face. Girl next-door type. Has calming effect on Jason and others. Good in a fight, brave to a fault. Pregnant. Mid 30s.

Chelsea – toddler, daughter of Jason and Carrie. Cute, rambunctious.

Kyle – Austin PD. Partner of Jason. Large man, built like a linebacker, with sandy blonde hair and a sly grin. Cheerful, funny, great in a fight, puts on front of being player, but really a romantic. Worships girlfriend Kate. Mid 30s.

Kate – strong, beautiful, emotional, witty. Former news reporter for a local Texas TV station. Fell hard for Kyle, carrying his baby. Temper. Early 30s.

Kelly – leader of Rednecks. Huge man with long brown hair and a beard. Tough, gruff, smart, great judge of character. Strategic thinker. Man's man. In love with Brenda. Mid 50s

Brenda – half-owner of Texas Mary's Bar and Grill in Dripping Springs. Voluptuous with bleach blonde hair and a slightly wild look. Deeply in love with Kelly. Extremely intelligent. Runs business side of Texas Mary's. Strong but worries about Kelly constantly. Good in a fight. Mid 50s.

Junior – Kelly's best friend. A tall rail of a man with a thick beard, usually wearing a battered cowboy hat. Funny, crazy, smarter than most people realize, good in a fight, strong, loyal to the death. In love with Rachel. Early 50s.

Rachel – picked up on the road. Black hair and brown eyes, short and thin, with a face of delicate beauty. Former drug abuser with difficult past. Lost only child to SIDS, which broke up her first marriage and led to the drug abuse. Leans on Junior, needs strong man in her life. Late 30s.

Curt – former police officer in Austin, and most recently San Antonio. Large man with a military haircut, clean shaven. Punched superior officer in San Antonio. Genius. Renaissance man. Understands many technical disciplines, creative, skilled. Has temper but with heart of gold. Likes to tease his friends. Would die for them. Skilled fighter who can turn the tide of a battle on his own. Sense of humor can be very crude but funny. Mid 40s.

Simon Orr – dangerous leader of militia movement, trying to take over Kelly's group. Large man wearing cowboy garb. Shadowy, cruel. Crossover character from original Bug Out! Series. Wants to become warlord. Playing against every side except his own. Mid 40s.

Sydney – one of the Merchant girls living outside of Fredericksburg, next to Jason's family homestead. Grew up with Jason and his brother Eric. Former teenage girlfriend of Eric. Beautiful, smart, funny, avid hunter and tracker, runs family moonshine business with her sister Amanda. Raven hair and stunning bright blue eyes. Mid 30s.

Amanda – Sydney's older sister. Raunchy, wild, aggressive, knows what she wants and goes for it hard. Beautiful, deep blue eyes like Sydney, hair bleached blond, contrasts with jet-black eyebrows. Tattoos. Smart, good negotiator, runs family moonshine business with Sydney, more technically savvy. Early 40s.

Gray – leader of the bikers, originally from southwest Texas. A large man with black hair and a black beard. Brave and resourceful, suspicious of strangers, but loyal once he's gained respect. Late 40s.

Cindy – Gray's wife. Nervous, small dainty blonde with tattoos and piercings. Pretty face ravaged by a hard life. Early 40s.

Moe – owner of the Fort Stockton RV Park. Overweight and balding with a gray and brown beard, shrewd and strong, strategic thinker, protective, kind. Mid 60s.

Clancy – Moe's nephew. Scraggly thin man with a wicked grin and long stringy brown hair. Works at the Fort Stockton RV Park. Smart as a whip with good intuition. Outdoorsman. Protective of the group, good with technology, good at organizing and getting things done. Mid-30s.

Brushy – owner of an RV Park overrun early in the story. He's been missing for a while. Small man with a huge beard and long hair, about sixty years old. Good in a fight, fearless, crazy, funny.

Pat – Brushy's sister, owner of the Amarillo Oasis RV Park. She's a couple years younger than Brushy, with a similar look. Short, robust, friendly, smart. Brave, angry at the invaders.

Jax – huge man with a blonde beard and a shaved head. Joined the group with a huge group of citizens. Gung ho, brave to a fault, cunning and loyal.

East Texas/Florida Group

Eric – Jason's brother. Over six feet tall with a trim but massive build. Was living in Florida before the war started. Private Investigator working elder fraud cases in retirement areas of central Florida. Brave, very athletic. Fast, good with guns and other weapons. Smart, charismatic. Loved by everybody. Loyal to a fault. Mid 30s.

Kim – Eric's girlfriend. Red-haired, freckled beauty with a slim build. Tough as nails but gentle, head over heels in love with Eric. Mid 30s.

Dirk – leader of Deadwood, Texas group. Medium sized man with a muscular build. Gruff, shrewd, brave, sentimental. Loves family and friends. Large man, muscular build. Late 50s, but a young late 50s.

Chance – best friend of Dirk. Short and chubby but quick, good in a fight. Wise cracks a lot. Good mixture of smarts and bravery, but cautious. Mid 40s.

Don – single dad widower with teenage daughter. Large man, average build with a conservative haircut. Kind and gentle, smart, protective. Lonely, misses wife. Brave but not really a fighter. Took in daughter's best friend when her family passed. Late 30s.

Francis – Don's older brother. Local political figure in Deadwood. Older man, spry for his age. Smart, good strategic thinker, understands the meaning of events better than rest of group, sage. Mid-60s.

Sherry – Francis's wife. Younger than him by ten years. Still pretty, trying hard to live during wartime but having trouble. Depression. Mid 50s.

Alyssa – Don's daughter. Pretty, a little self-centered. Misses mother. Terrified of enemy after attacks on Deadwood. 17 years old.

Chloe – Alyssa's best friend. Orphan taken in by Don after both parents killed. Mousey, kind, smart, helps Alyssa to cope. 17 years old.

Alex – Owner of the MidPoint 66 Café, who met the group during the I-40 battle. Older man, bald and heavy set, robust, funny.

Kitten – Daughter of Alex. Middle aged, chubby with light brown hair and a pretty face. Waitress at her father's Café.

Stanton Hunt – War Chief of the Mescalero Tribe. Brave man, thoughtful, severed in the Army for years, friends with General Hogan.

White Eagle – adviser and spokesperson for the Mescalero Tribe. Doesn't trust the white man. In favor of keeping an alliance with the Islamists. Dangerous man.

DPS Patrol Boaters Group

Juan Carlos – young, handsome Hispanic, full of vigor and enthusiasm. Skilled boat pilot, brave and cunning. Family in Texas since before the Alamo. Loves the state, patriot. Mid 20s.

Brendan – partner of Juan Carlos. Also young and handsome, ginger redhead. Loves to joke and tease, but can be serious. Good with weapons, natural fighter. Mid 20s.

Lieutenant Richardson – Leader of Juan Carlos and Brendan. Handsome man of average size and build with light brown hair. Tough, strong, thoughtful, loyal, brave. Headed for higher rank. Mid 30s.

Lita – girlfriend of Lieutenant Richardson. Beautiful Hispanic woman with model's figure and expressive eyes. Witty, smart, brave. Emotional, worships her man. Protective, mothering. Mid 30s.

Madison – girlfriend of Juan Carlos. Emotional but brave, beautiful with thick blonde hair and curvy figure, college girl forced to quit due to war. Head over heels for Juan Carlos. Mid 20s.

Hannah – best friend of Madison and girlfriend of Brendan. Dark haired beauty. Slim dancer's figure, athletic. Self-conscious, afraid to be hurt, passionate, very deeply in love with Brendan. Can rally in a fight if needed, surprisingly brave when pushed. Terrified of losing Brendan in the war. Mid 20s.

DPS Commissioner Wallace – overall head of DPS Organization. Strong, cunning, thinks several steps ahead of most others. Black man, large and imposing. Loves his men. Feeling is mutual. Early 60s.

Chuck – Gun shop owner in downtown San Antonio, Texas. Big man, brave, expert gunsmith. In love with Carol.

Roberto – owner of a property near Purgatory Creek. Large Mexican man, middle aged, with a good heart, brave but cautious.

Kris – small white woman with gray hair, middle aged, married to Roberto. Brave and strong, used to hardship from childhood. Generous and loving.

Gerald – Roberto's friend. Redneck always ready for a fight. Long gray hair, thin, always wearing a railroad cap. Brave to a fault.

Jay – Roberto's friend, and friends with Gerald. Lanky black-haired man in his early fifties. Sensitive but will fight hard when pushed.

Hector – Another friend of Roberto's. Overweight Mexican man in his mid-forties. A little crazy. Demolition expert. Always ready to bring dynamite to any party.

Harley – DPS Lieutenant, stationed at the new South Padre Island base. Good man with goofy sense of humor and an easygoing manner.

Leadership

Kip Hendrix – President Pro Tempore of the Texas Senate, and the leading liberal in that body. Large man, bald, with a wrinkled face but a dashing look. Has corrupt past, problems with sexual harassment, but down deep has a good heart. Trying to be better. Very complex person. Old friends with Governor, loves him even though they were estranged for many years. Multi-level thinker, good intuition, protective of those he loves, nasty enemy to have. Deeply in love with Maria, although he viewed her as just another conquest at first. Early 50s.

Maria – secretary to Kip Hendrix. Hispanic beauty with curvy figure and a haunting face, well liked and respected by all around her. Knows how to get things done in Texas government. Fell hard for Kip Hendrix, now loyal to him above all else. Late 30s.

Governor Nelson – Charismatic conservative leader of Texas. Handsome in a rugged way. Patriotic, honest, strong, but opinionated. Old college buddy with Kip Hendrix. Strong bonds between them, even though they are political opposites. Thinks several steps ahead of others, takes risks when he knows he's right. Loved by the people of Texas, for the most part. Has solid-gold BS detector. Early 50s.

Brian – Governor Nelson's secretary and right-hand man. Black man. Cunning and loyal to the Governor. Protects him at all times. Much more important person than most people know. Mid 30s.

Commissioner Holly – ultra left-wing member of the Police Commission. Friends with Kip Hendrix. Tall and skinny with a goatee. Smart but far from open-minded. Constantly knocking heads with the Austin Police Department. Holding his nose to support Governor Nelson while the war is on. Mid 50s.

Jerry Sutton – aid to Kip Hendrix. Political operator. Clean shaven and pudgy. Tries to do a good job. Cares more about power than political philosophy. Early 30s.

Chief Ramsey – Austin Police Chief. Overweight but still burley, with the look of a redneck. Old friends with Governor Nelson. Didn't get along with Kip Hendrix in the past, but friends now, fighting a common enemy. Brave and loyal, strong leader, cares more about his cops than himself. Early 50s.

Major General Gallagher – head of Texas Army National Guard. Old-time soldier, tough and strong, unafraid. Loved by his men. Mid 60s.

Major General Landry – head of Texas Air National Guard. Cocky but cautious about using his resources, almost to a fault. Late 40s.

General Walker – US Army General, stationed in Texas until the war broke out. Near genius intelligence, charismatic, uncanny ability to turn a defeat into a victory. Feared by the enemy. Crossover character from original Bug Out! Series. Mid 50s.

General Hogan – US Army General, friend of General Walker. Black man, loved by his men, tough, no-nonsense. Strategic thinker, takes risks, understands people. Fine leader. Crossover character from original Bug Out! Series. Mid 50s.

Saladin – evil leader of the Islamist forces in the western states. He is not in Texas, but the Texas leadership is aware of him and his plans. Crossover character from original Bug Out! Series.

President Simpson – current President of the United States.

Major Josh Carlson – Second in command over the Texas Air National Guard. Right Hand Man of Major General Landry.

Celia – beautiful but troubled sister of Maria. Mental issues; depression and addiction.

Private Ken Brown – General Hogan's son. On special assignment to help the Fort Stockton team.

Private Jose Sanchez – on General Hogan's staff. Childhood friend of Private Brown. On special assignment to help the Fort Stockton team.

Captain Smith – near genius Texas Army National Guard officer with rank of Captain. Pilots effort to mass-produce Curt's gimbal system for vehicles. Designs adjustable mounts for mini-guns.

ABOUT THE AUTHOR

Robert G Boren is a writer from the South Bay section of Southern California. He writes Short Stories, Novels, and Serialized Fiction.

Made in the USA
Las Vegas, NV
09 April 2021